SLAYING ON THE LAKE SHORE

A VIKING WITCH MYSTERY

CATE MARTIN

CHAPTER ONE

IN SOME PARTS of the world, March might be the beginning of spring, but on the shores of Lake Superior, it is still very much winter. The sun is higher in the sky, and the days are longer, but none of that seems to be enough to warm the bones.

Take Frór's cabin, where my grandmother and I were staying as she recovered from overusing her magic. The cabin walls were of sturdy stone, the thick glass windows tight, and every room kept warm by its own fireplace.

But that was because it had to be. Frór had built it on a promontory of rock that jutted out over the cold water. We were dozens of feet above lake level, but the chill Superior winds still whipped around us on three sides. If anything, they were stronger because of the height.

You had to watch your hat on good days. On bad days, you had to watch for waves. Yes, even nearly a hundred feet up. It was too cold to mess with even a bit of spray wetting your clothes, but walls of water washing over the yard weren't unheard of either.

Not that I had seen it. The weather hadn't been bad at all for as long as my grandmother and I had been there. It hadn't been warm or particularly sunny, but there had been no bad storms either. No drifts of snow taller than I was barricading the door or blinding winds making walking into town too risky because the road was so hard to keep in sight.

But it was cold. Cold and gray. And not a lot of fun to draw.

But even that was okay for me. I hadn't done a lot of drawing from my imagination since leaving St. Paul for Runde and the Viking-era village of Villmark that hid beyond Runde. There had been so much to see and sketch around me, I had just never gotten back to drawing my more customary illustrations of Norse myths and legends.

Now I had a nice stack of finished work to add to my portfolio. And another stack of pen and ink drawings of the landscapes of the North Shore for my friend Jessica to sell for me in her café.

All I needed to do was get them to her.

But I had no idea when I'd be able to get back to Runde. It depended on my grandmother.

I looked up from my work at my easel to where my grandmother sat in the window seat across the room from me. She was curled up in a woolen blanket, a mug of spiced cider in her hands, and a book spread open across her knees. My polydactyl black cat, Mjolner, was curled up sleeping on the window seat near her feet.

But her eyes were, as they all too often were these days, staring out across the gray waters of the lake to the equally gray horizon beyond. Although they had an unfocused look, as if she wasn't really seeing any of that, anyway.

Even her customary long braid of thick white hair was more loosely woven as it draped forward over her shoulder. Not untidy, just very relaxed. Which was weird for my grandmother. I was used to watching her run two towns in two different worlds, not chilling out with a good book.

I sighed, filling my lungs with the fresh smell of wood smoke from the fireplace, a lovely smell that still never quite conquered the underlying mustiness of the old cabin. I picked up my mug and drained the last of my own measure of spiced cider. The apples used had been so tart that drinking the cider almost made me more thirsty than I had been before. But the sweetness combined with the spiciness of the cinnamon and ginger and cloves was warming.

At least, when I remembered to drink it before it got chilled, like it had now.

The pan of cider was still on the stove, gently simmering, but I opted not to get myself a second mug. The sun was dipping low in the sky, and it was nearly time for my evening walk.

"Mormor, do you want a warm up?" I asked her. She took a long moment to tear her eyes away from the window before giving me a puzzled look. But then she glanced down at her nearly empty mug before holding it out for me.

"Yes, thank you, Ingrid," she said. Then she looked down at the book on her lap as if its presence confused her as well.

"I'll put what's left of last night's soup on the back burner before I go so we can eat when I get back," I said as I poured the last of the cider into her mug, then brought it back to her.

It was a small cabin, one multifunction room below and three tiny bedrooms in a row across the loft above, but I didn't mind it. My grandmother was easy to spend a day with. She had a sixth sense for when I was in the flow with my work and shouldn't be disturbed, and when I was just going through the motions, or doing something fussy but not too mentally taxing when I could both draw and carry on a conversation at once.

Maybe you'd have to be an artist yourself to understand how amazing and rare that ability is. But she had it in spades.

My grandmother took the mug of cider from me and brought it close to her face to inhale the spices with a smile, but she didn't yet take a sip. "How is Andrew doing?" she asked me instead.

"Everyone in Runde is doing great," I told her. "Of course they wonder when we'll be back, but they understand these things take time."

I thought that was a pretty solid hint, but when my grandmother just hmmed and went back to staring out the window, I knew I had been too subtle.

To my semitrained eyes, my grandmother seemed entirely recovered from where she had been after the spells on her mead hall had come crashing down. I couldn't imagine what more had to happen before we could go home.

But my grandmother had been dodging even direct inquiries into how she was doing, so I had stopped asking. She would be ready when she was ready, and in the meantime, I had my studies in magic and my art to pass the time.

But I couldn't shake the feeling that she *was* completely recovered. That she wasn't waiting to feel well again, because she already was well.

That she was waiting for something else.

But I didn't know what that might be.

So I just took the container of leftover soup out of our rudimentary icebox and poured it into the cast-iron pot that always sat on the back burner of the gas stove. I left it on the lowest possible simmer, then headed to the mudroom to get all my wind-proof layers on before heading out into the fading day.

Mjolner lifted his head to look at me briefly. Then he resumed his nap. I couldn't blame him. He looked really cozy there with my grandmother.

The wind hit me at once, chapping the skin of my already reddened cheeks and nipping at my ears. I pulled my wool hat lower to cover my earlobes, then turned away from the road that led from town straight to our front door to follow a narrower track that worked its way down to the shore in a series of steep switch-backs.

Since the promontory jutted out almost directly eastward, I was out of the rays of the setting sun the minute I started down the first leg of the path. But I was only getting the wind from two directions now and not three. Believe me, that made a difference. My hat stayed on, and my hood stayed up over it, with both my hands free in case I stumbled on the path.

Which happened more than I'd like to admit. The rocks could get icy, but you'd never know it to look at them. It was a pretty treacherous walk to take every single afternoon.

But the shore below was the only place my cellphone could catch a signal. And that was my only lifeline to my Runde friends.

I could see ships on the horizon as I walked. Most were following the routes of cargo ships on Lake Superior, but others were of a different kind all together. Ocean-faring ships, and not modern ones.

Not that I could see the details from so far out. But I could smell the salty tang of seawater and hear the calls of unfamiliar birds. The magic of this place connected a few different places. At least one had an ocean coast, but I had no idea which one. Not even my grandmother knew.

Some months ago and quite a bit further inland, I had walked part of a road that led up into distant mountains and eventually to Old Norway, if only a very small part of that road. And I had watched my friend Thorbjorn and his four brothers fight trolls on a hillside that had felt like Icelandic volcanic ground to me. But I had no clue how to tell one body of water from another. Maybe if I caught a fish.

I was distracted from my thoughts by the sudden buzzing of my phone in my back pocket. I didn't take it out. The closer I got to the shore, the icier the path became and the more I needed to stay alert with my hands at the ready. But I counted the buzzes. A lot of texts since I had been down here last the day before.

I smiled. My friends missed me. Which was nice. Because I really missed them.

At last I reached the shore. The waves were pretty calm at the moment, but even that was enough to leave a cold mist in the air. My windbreaker kept me dry until I found the nook in the cliff-side where my favorite sitting rock waited for me. Out of the wind, mostly out of the mist, and smooth enough to be comfortable if a bit cold.

I settled in and finally took out my phone. All the texts were from Andrew, and I had a feeling I knew what they would be about before I even had my password typed in.

Sure enough, the shadow box job he had agreed to do for Jessica had developed yet another wrinkle.

I grinned as I scrolled through the texts. I had been in a similar place in a job I had done once for a friend, doing illustrations on spec for a children's book they had never actually published in the end. Jessica, like my writer friend, had given only a vague idea of what they were looking for, promising that whatever was delivered would surely be perfect, because Andrew, like me, was a talented artist.

But with every conversation since it became more and more clear that Jessica, like my writer friend, had very specific ideas about what they wanted. They just weren't very good at communicating them.

So I felt Andrew's pain. I had no idea that Jessica, who always seemed so laid back, was at the core a bit of a control freak. But I suppose you'd have to be to run your own business at twenty-four.

He had included photos of the boxes he had made so far, and they were really lovely. Jessica wanted to put little knickknacks in them, antique souvenirs her mother had collected over the years from different places up and down the North Shore. What Andrew was doing—using found wood he sourced locally, each piece having a whole story behind it about where the wood came from and how it had been used before it had become a shadow box—was really quite cool.

"If she makes you start from scratch, I'll buy those from you," I texted him. I didn't know what I'd do with them. They were far too small for art supplies to fit in them, but I could take up miniature painting or something. I even knew just where I'd hang them in my Villmark house.

"I just might take you up on that," Andrew texted back, with an eye-roll emoji.

"How's she doing otherwise?" I texted, then waited. I had a single bar here when I had any at all, and making an actual phone call had proven impossible the couple of times we had tried it. For his part, Andrew had to walk out to a particular stretch of shoreline near his house, so both of us were outside now, under the same darkening skies.

"She's good. Michelle too. Loke says you're good when he sees you?" he answered.

I chuckled, then typed. "You're wise to doubt him. It's been more than two weeks since he was last here. I have a stack of drawings for Jessica's café, but no way to get them to her."

"Send me pics," he texted back at once.

I scrolled through my photos. I hadn't taken pictures of them all, but I had one or two. I picked one I particularly liked of Freya in her chariot drawn by Norwegian forest cats.

"Hope this works," I texted, because for whatever reason he had a better time sending pics my way than the other way around.

And indeed, the text with the photo didn't go through. And that one bar disappeared entirely.

I sighed and put my phone away. The stars were coming out already, but it felt like we'd barely spoken to each other. So much time was lost waiting for the messages to get across to each other. It was frustrating.

But I reminded myself this was just one moment in time. Eventually, it would end.

Even if it did feel like I'd pressed pause on my life just when it was getting interesting.

Without the phone to distract me, the stone underneath me suddenly seemed much colder. I slid down off the rock, but my eyes were up on the sky. The stars shone brightly, the clouds that had been thick for days finally breaking apart and exposing large swaths of indigo skies.

Somewhere to the south of me, Andrew was probably looking up at them, too. If only I could get them to carry messages for me.

I snugged my jacket hood more tightly over my woolen hat, then started the long slog back up the promontory to the cabin above.

CHAPTER TWO

ᚠ

THE NEXT DAY WAS WEDNESDAY, the day someone always brought us supplies from Villmark.

That "someone" was supposed to be Loke and Roarr. They had volunteered for it. And for the first two weeks, they had come through.

Then on week three, it was just Roarr on his own with a vague story about Loke being tied up with something else. I didn't mind the lie. I knew Loke's sister was often unwell, and I also knew that Loke didn't like to talk about his family with others. I figured he had told a tale that I would see the truth in, but wouldn't require him to let Roarr in on the secret.

Then, on the fourth week, neither of them had turned up. Instead, two Villmarker young men had guided the ox cart up the track. I hadn't recognized either of them, and they hadn't offered their names.

They weren't as openly unfriendly as Raggi and his friends who advocated for a Villmark that never interacted with Runde at all. Those guys resented my grandmother and me both, although more so me since I had grown up outside of Villmark and only recently returned. But they weren't exactly friendly either.

They had a similarly vague story about Loke's absence, but neither of them knew anything about what was going on with Roarr. Perhaps he had just grown bored with a tiresome chore.

So as I walked out to the crossroads at the head of the promontory for the fifth time, I had no idea who I was actually waiting for. If it were finally Loke again, or even just Roarr, I could give either of them my drawings to deliver to Jessica. But I didn't bother getting my hopes up.

I left the wind and crash of waves behind me as I followed the road towards the mainland. As always, I felt an uneasiness in my stomach as I crossed the narrowest part of the promontory, where the rock was barely wider than the path. Eventually, all of this would give in to the wind and waves and fall away. A big chunk of Pictured Rocks on the Michigan side had fallen into the lake just a few summers ago. As much as that was almost certainly centuries away from happening here, if not millennia, I still hated walking across that particular bit.

Geological changes aside, it felt too much like a sudden burst of wind could carry me away. And it was a very long way down to a brutally rocky shore below. Long enough, I feared, time enough to regret tripping before meeting the rocks.

But after that narrow point, I was out on solid ground. The meadows around me were still snow-covered, but the hardy birch trees that dotted the side of the road here and there had shaken off their own white mantles. Their grayish-white branches reached up to the clear blue sky, as if stretching out before getting to the real work of growing green buds.

Soon. It would be spring soon.

I reached the point where the road to the cabin branched off from the main road that hugged the coast from the meadow over Runde to unimaginably distant points to the north, where the magic was stronger.

There was a stone marker set by the side of the road, although if it had ever had any writing on it, that had been worn smooth long ago. It wasn't large enough to sit on, but I stood beside it, leaning on the walking stick I had brought with me, and scanned the world around me for signs of life.

I saw someone walking from one patch of woods to another, but the gentle rolling of a few hills between me and them obscured all but their bright green hat. But it didn't matter. I knew who I was looking at.

It was Leifr, the boy who had been lost as a child and returned as a rather disturbed youth. He lived in the hidden village outside of Villmark, where the refugees who had returned from the modern world kept their own separate community. He lived with Signi, who had been a psychiatrist during her time in the modern world and still wrote articles from time to time.

I had never actually met him, but I was sure it was him. Villmarkers seldom came this far north, and never alone. But from what I had heard from others, Leifr had no fear of what lurked in the north. He might have been trapped there, but he hadn't been helpless.

Having a chat with him when I was back in Villmark was pretty high on my wishlist. But since coming out to the cabin, I had seen him from afar pretty much every time I had walked out to these meadows. The boy was restless, that was for sure.

I raised a hand in greeting, but as usual, he didn't seem to notice me. Or he didn't want me to know he saw me. I didn't know if he was shy or people-averse or if Signi just felt it was best to keep him away from others while she treated him for the trauma of his misplaced childhood.

I really wanted to talk to him.

"He sees you. I guess he just doesn't like you," a voice said out of nowhere in strongly accented Villmarker Norse. I jumped and yelped, spinning to see an old man standing with feet spread wide as if guarding the path to the north behind me as I had gazed to the south. He had a long, twisted staff planted on the ground in front of him, and the wind from the lake was whipping at his long cloak and the equally long garments he wore beneath. His battered, wide-brimmed hat was pulled low against that wind, and his face was mostly in shadow. All I could discern was a silvery-gray beard so long he wore it tucked into his belt.

More unsettling, he seemed to have only one eye. One eye that glinted too brightly out of the shadow under his hat brim.

"Do I know you?" I asked, more rudely than I had intended.

"I should hope so!" he said gruffly, but didn't go on to identify himself at all. If I had ever met him before in Villmark as an adult or during my childhood summer spent there, I couldn't recall him at all. And he looked like someone I would definitely remember.

"Do you know me?" I asked.

"Lost daughter of the oldest line. Scribbler of silliness. Dabbler in danger. Amateur wielder of paltry powers. Half-literate misinterpreter of runes. Or, if you will, Ingrid Torfudottir," he said, ending with a dismissive huff of breath.

My blood burned. But there was nothing I could say that wasn't going to sound childishly defensive.

I mean, he was actually pretty accurate. Cruel, but accurate.

"As if your presence weren't ruination enough of this fine spring day, here come these two layabouts. Wastes of space. Dodgers of dangerous crimes," he grumbled, far too loud to be speaking to himself.

I turned to look south again and saw the ox-cart of supplies just emerging from the wood on the far side of the meadow. A single ox plodded along at the yoke, head down as it worked. Walking on either side of it, minding the wheels as they tumbled in and out of the road's many ruts, were Loke and Roarr.

I turned back to the strange old man, still nameless in my mind. "What crimes are these?" I asked.

He just scoffed out another breath, as if the question was beneath his dignity to answer.

I left him standing there to run to the cart. Loke was underdressed as usual, in shirtsleeves with no hat. The wind tousled the waves of his chocolate brown hair but brought not a hint of color to his pale cheeks. And, as always, he was dressed all in black.

Roarr at least was dressed for the weather, if more like a Runde fisherman in modern work boots and a waterproof down jacket than the Villmarker he was.

"It's about time you turned back up," I said to Loke as soon as I was close enough to be heard. "I have a stack of drawings for you to take back to Jessica. As you promised."

"I know," he said. "Roarr and I are back on the job now."

"For this week, anyway," I grumbled.

"For as many weeks as it takes," Roarr swore dutifully.

But Loke was grinning at me. "How many weeks, do you think?"

"I have no idea," I admitted. "She seems better. And yet she never speaks of going home. Does someone from the council have to come out here and examine her first or something?"

"Gah, I hope not," Loke said with a grimace. "No one could know better than Nora when she's recovered. And no one is less inclined to lie about the state of things than she is either."

"She hid how poorly she was doing for a long time," Roarr pointed out, then gave me an apologetic look.

"No, you're right," I said. I was about to say more when Loke finally noticed the old man still standing in the middle of the road south of the fork.

"What's *he* doing here?" he asked in a harsh whisper.

"Whatever he pleases, Loke Grímsson," the man said, his voice booming over the whistle of the wind.

How had he even heard what Loke had said? It didn't seem possible over that distance. But I had seen stranger things since discovering Villmark.

"Who is he?" I asked Loke.

"His name is Odd Oddsen," Loke told me. "Some claim he was among the first settlers who came over from Norway with Torfa. And by 'some' I mean 'him'. He claims that."

It wasn't hard to tell that Loke didn't believe this was true. It didn't mesh with anything I'd learned in my magical studies, either. If living such an extended life were possible, surely my ancestress Torfa would've done it herself.

Unless it had taken all of her power just to protect Villmark. Although what she was protecting it from, I still didn't know.

There was so much I still didn't know.

Odd didn't speak to us again, but to my immediate displeasure he fell in step behind the ox-cart when we turned it towards the cabin. As annoying as the thought of him always guarding the northern road was, the idea of him being in the cozy cabin I shared amiably with my grandmother was even worse.

But as we drew closer, I saw my grandmother dressed in her warmest coat standing outside the cabin door. She had a wool hat pulled low over her head, and she was casually sipping at a mug of coffee as she watched us approach. But her white braid was once more down the center of her back, and very tightly plaited.

She wasn't waiting for us. I knew that in my bones. She was waiting for this Odd fellow. And she had braided her hair like a Valkyrie expecting battle.

"Nora," Odd called, touching the brim of his hat as he approached.

"Odd," she returned with the slightest of nods. "Ingrid is staying in your usual bedroom, but I'm sure you'll have no objection to the northern-most room." That last had a ring of command to it. She would brook no objections.

Odd grumbled to himself, but just nodded and pushed his way inside the cabin.

"He thinks I know him," I said to my grandmother. "I don't remember him at all."

"Not all your memories of your childhood days here have returned," she reminded me. But then she frowned. "Even so, I don't recall the two of you ever meeting. Odd always comes back to Vill-mark, but years go by between visits. Your time here was in one of those gaps."

"But he knows me," I said, and to my horror, heard how strangled those words sounded. My throat was too tight. But his assessment of me had really hurt.

Which was weird. As an artist, I knew how to deal with rejection, even brutal rejection. But this felt different. Why?

"He knows *of* you," she said. "Try not to let him disturb you too much. His visits are always short. Short, but troublesome."

I looked over to where Roarr and Loke were working together, unloading crates of food from the back of the cart and stacking it by the door for me to bring inside later. I stepped closer to my grandmother to whisper, "Loke says he's one of the first settlers here. Like, from the time of Torfa?"

"So people say," she said, more whimsically than I would've liked.

"Is it true?" I asked.

But she just smiled at me and shrugged, then went inside the cabin.

"Someday you'll be like that," Loke said with a grin. "All maddeningly vague answers and knowing smiles."

"You're one to talk," I shot back, then took the crate of milk bottles he held out to me to carry it inside the house.

I hoped my grandmother was right, that this Odd fellow's visit would be short.

But I was afraid her second prediction would prove right as well. That his visit would be troublesome. The mood inside the cabin was already inverting the world outside. While the sky had gone from stormy to clear, the homeyness of our snug little cabin had become downright claustrophobic.

I could see a lot more walks in my future.

CHAPTER THREE

Luckily for me, getting the supplies wasn't the only task I had on my list for Wednesday. After putting everything away and sweeping all the clumps of snow we had dragged in back out of the mudroom, I put my jacket and hat back on and headed back out to the road.

But this time I kept going, following the southern branch back towards Villmark.

But not all the way to the town proper. No, my destination was my own second home, tucked away in the woods just north of town.

Imagine, a starving artist with two gorgeous homes on the North Shore. I'm lucky, I know.

This one was a cottage in a clearing left to me by an artist who had turned out to be a murderer. I had caught him with the help of Thorbjorn and his brothers. His trial on the hilltop with an audience of trolls had been my first act as my grandmother's eventual successor as volva of Villmark. A volva is a witch, adviser to the council, and in certain cases, judge over criminal cases.

I could have brought the artist Solvi back to Villmark, or even to Runde, to face the justice of the modern world. But in the end I had elected to let him keep walking ever northward.

Maybe he had reached Old Norway or was still on his way. But it was far more likely he had died not soon after I had lost sight of him.

But for reasons I don't quite understand, he had left me his home. And what a home it was. Even this deep in winter where the snow is more gray and dirty than sparkling white and pure, the clearing around the cottage looked like a winter wonderland version of a sculpture garden. The bear carved from a tree trunk was the largest, but the many little trolls were my favorites.

The exterior of the cabin, too, was a work of art. The patterns in the wood brought out by his skilled hand to suggest the motion of water of the lake now out of sight but never far out of my mind were gorgeous. Even more so was the central pillar of the cottage carved to resemble the World Tree Yggdrasil.

No, not resemble. That's too small a word. He had carved it to tell its story, which was really every story, every nuance of every tale. I had yet to spend enough time in the cottage to find all the details I knew were there, snuggled among the carved leaves overhead.

But I was there for a purpose, and it wasn't admiring the woodwork. It was too cold inside to take off my jacket or hat yet, but I quickly built a fire in the stone fireplace. I knew from experience that would warm the whole space faster than seemed possible.

I had to break a sizable crust of ice off the water barrel outside my door before I was able to fill the kettle, but soon I had that settled over the now-roaring fire. While I waited for it to come to a boil, I opened my pack and took out the tea things I had brought with me from the cabin as well as a loaf of dark bread, a wheel of pale white cheese, and a couple of apples and pears. A nice little lunch for two.

I was just hanging up my coat and hat when I glanced out the window and saw a stooped form making its way through the snow to my door.

"Haraldr!" I said as I threw the door open. He looked up, pushing his woolen hood back until I could see his eyes.

"Greetings, Ingrid Torfudottir. It has been an age!" he said as he continued his limping walk up to my door.

"Are you all right?" I asked. He always walked with a limp and a stick, but the limp had never been so pronounced.

"Quite fine, quite fine," he assured me. "This is a hard season for me, late winter. Every year is like this. The cold and my old joints. But every day is a little warmer than the last. Such is the way of things. Now, I know you said you'd bring everything for lunch, but I couldn't help bringing one of Ullr's famous elk sausages with me. I hope you don't mind."

"No, that sounds lovely," I said as he pressed a paper-wrapped bundle into my hands. I peeled back the paper to see a long, dark sausage that smelled strongly of fennel and juniper. "And it smells divine," I quickly added. "Eat first or the lesson?" I asked.

"Eat first, of course," Haraldr said with a laugh.

Once we'd had three cups of tea apiece and as much food as we could stuff in, I had heard pretty much all the news of Villmark. Loke was never as forthcoming as Andrew, so my knowledge of how things were going in Runde was far more complete than that of Villmark despite the latter being so much closer to me.

"I'm sorry to hear that Kara is still feeling down," I said. "I wish she could come and see us at the cabin. I think she'd enjoy a few days there with us."

"I'm sure she would, but she and her sister are quite busy. They are, after all, trying to take the place of five Thors," Haraldr said. But then his tone grew even more serious. "I had hoped that keeping busy would keep her mind occupied, but now I fear guarding the ancestral flame leaves her too much time to brood and miss her man."

I wondered if Kara thought of it like that, like Thorge was her man. Something had definitely changed between them while I was lost in the woods, fleeing the Wild Hunt. When I had left the hunting lodge where we had all been staying, the two of them had been just warmly friendly, no more.

But when we had stood side by side watching the Thors march off to the north and she had squeezed my hand in hers so tightly? Something had definitely changed.

But I could no more go to Villmark to talk to her about it than she could come out to the cabin to talk to me. I was meant to be watching over my grandmother. Being this close to Villmark now was an exception Haraldr had insisted on.

It had been far too long since my last lesson. And I suspected that worsening limp of his was why he hadn't made the walk out to the cabin himself.

"So," I said in a slow drawl, "before we get to the lesson, I did have something I wanted to ask you about. I asked my grandmother, but she didn't quite answer me."

"I don't know what I could tell you that you grandmother could not, but I shall do my best," Haraldr said.

"Well, I don't think it was so much that she couldn't as that she chose not to," I said. "It's about the man who turned up today. Odd Oddsen."

"Oh, him," Haraldr said. He made no effort to hide how unthrilled he was to hear that name. "I suppose he told you he's been here since the beginning?"

"No, it was Loke that mentioned that," I said. "But that wasn't even the most puzzling thing. I know I've never met him, but he seemed to know a lot about me. If he's been in the north since before I returned, how could he?"

"He has his ways," Haraldr said.

Loke was right. All the old ones with any knowledge of magic at all constantly fell back on the maddeningly vague.

"It's not important at this time," he said, so I guessed some of what I was thinking had been showing on my face.

"I also had a request," I said. Haraldr nodded as he used a fingertip to gather up crumbs from his plate. "I know this is a onetime arrangement, meeting here, but I was hoping if we could make it two, I would really like to meet that boy, Leifr."

"Leifr?" Haraldr repeated, caught off guard.

"I've seen him wandering everywhere north of Villmark. I'm curious to hear his story," I said.

"I'm not sure he's ready for that," Haraldr said. "Most of what happened to him he still hasn't told even to Signi. And she is adamant that we must not press him. No one wants to lock him up or hold him against his will, but that means his fleeing all of us is always a risk."

"Is he dangerous?" I asked.

"Only possibly to himself," Haraldr said. "When he is ready to talk to others, I will ask Signi to let you speak with him. Is that satisfactory?"

"Of course," I said.

"And Nora?" Haraldr asked.

I sighed. "I really wished one of you would come out to the cabin and see for yourself. Ask her for yourself. She won't tell me anything, so I can only tell you what I see and think. Which really isn't what anyone should be making decisions based on."

"True, but the one making the decision is Nora herself. I am merely curious," he assured me.

"Then I think she is quite recovered. I think she's so well she's growing bored. But for whatever reason, we are still there at the cabin. I almost wonder if she's waiting for something."

"Perhaps," Haraldr said. "Don't fret too much. She will tell you in time. After so many years guiding so many souls in our village as well as the modern one, I'm sure these days with no one demanding anything of her, with only you for company, are a balm to her. Don't rush her to come back."

"I won't. I haven't," I said, but I felt my cheeks flushing. I hadn't said a word to my grandmother about it, that was true. But I had been wishing she would get a move on for some time now.

"Now, the lesson?" Haraldr asked. At my nod, he pushed his empty plate away and reached into his satchel to set a single charcoal drawing on a scrap of heavy paper on the crumb-strewn tabletop.

Another rune, of course. This one looked like someone had turned a capital F into a sort of flag. The arms swooped downward from the flagpole, then briefly up again at the ends.

"Ase," I said.

"Correct," Haraldr said, sitting back and folding his hands over his full belly. "We have worked our way through all the chaos after creation. Here, finally, we reach the first rune that represents order."

"I could've used a little order when I was dealing with that Mandy woman," I said with a shudder.

"Perhaps," he allowed. "But I feel the timing is perfect now. You see, this rune also represents the knowledge that is passed down to us from our ancestors. Such as from your grandmother to you."

"We haven't done any magic together since we got to the cabin," I admitted.

"No, but as she recovers, she will surely ask you to," Haraldr said. "Delving into this rune now will make you better prepared."

"Maybe," I said. I traced the shape with a fingertip over the charcoal. "Something about this feels familiar. I mean, I know the letter sounds for every rune from my drawing. But this is different."

"Ah," Haraldr said, his eyes suddenly bright. "Perhaps because this is the rune of Odin, and particularly Odin in his guise as the leader of the Wild Hunt."

"Please tell me I'm not in any danger of summoning that by mistake," I said. Just the words "Wild Hunt" had sent a cold shiver up my spine.

"I can't promise any such thing," he said almost gleefully. "But I think it is more likely you will touch his other aspects as you study this. Odin is the lord of the dead in that Wild Hunt persona, but his other persona connects with magic and ecstasy, and knowledge gained by such means."

"I'm not sure I like the sound of that any better," I admitted. "It sounds... out of control."

"Perhaps," he said. Then he sat quietly, waiting for me to speak again.

"It looks like a flag in the wind," I said. It sounded lame in my own ears, but he just gave me another of those happy smiles.

"Air, wind, breath-itself," he said. "But not just that, the unseen. It is also sound. The sounds of nature, the sounds of communication of animals and humans. But above all, it is the language of symbols like the runes themselves. It is the rune of poetry."

"That's a lot of stuff packed into one rune," I said. I wasn't sure how

I was going to meditate on so much at once. Just the idea of it was overwhelming.

Plus, the unseen movement of wind might be something I could draw by how it affected things like flags and cloaks. But poetry? Even the most image-intensive poetry was not really something I could reach for with my own visual arts.

This was going to be tricky.

"This sounds a little outside of my wheelhouse," I admitted.

"Don't let it intimidate you. Believe me, no matter the guise he chooses, Odin loves to intimidate you. But he's just a god," Haraldr said.

"Just a god?" I repeated.

"Our gods are not like others. They strive higher and harder than mere mortals, but they are not omnipotent, and what they gain is not without cost."

"Yeah, I can think of a few stories," I said. Specifically, I thought of Odin hanging for days from the World Tree before flying off in a raving madness, but with the knowledge of the runes now in his possession.

If I turned my head, I could probably find a little carving of that moment in the roof of my cottage.

"I think this is very much in your wheelhouse," Haraldr said, carefully repeating my own words back to me. I was pretty sure he knew what a wheelhouse was, but the expression was probably new to him. "This rune isn't Thurs, with all of its brute force. This is a rune of soft and cunning power. That sounds like your style."

"Soft maybe," I mumbled. I wasn't sure I would describe myself as cunning. I wasn't even sure I wanted to.

"It's about opening up your subconscious, to allow your mind to be a conduit for an artistic inspiration. Odin chose poetry. But your art is your conduit."

"Perhaps when I try meditating on it, it will start to make more sense," I said. In the past, the other runes had eventually become clear in my mind. But what if I really was more comfortable in chaos than in order?

That was a chilling thought. So chilling I didn't dare speak it aloud to Haraldr. As close as we'd become over the last few months, he was still a member of the council. And that council held my fate in their hands. Saying I felt more comfortable with chaos than order wasn't going to help improve their view of me as an outsider and meddler at all.

"Just open up your mind," he said, spreading his hands out on either side of his head as if demonstrating this. Then he got up from the table and started wrapping up the last of the sausage we hadn't managed to eat. "I will speak to Signi about Leifr for you, and I'll let you know what she says. But no promises." Then a thought struck him as he was pulling up his hood and he let it drop again to give me a curious look. "Have you seen magic around him? When you see him walking near the cabin?"

"It never occurred to me to even look," I admitted. "I don't generally carry my wand with me when I leave the cabin. Perhaps I should."

"Of course you should," he said sternly. "And not so you can use it to look at Leifr. That was a gift given to protect you. How can it protect you if you don't have it on you when you need it?"

I had never seen anything remotely threatening anywhere near the cabin except the lake itself and perhaps Odd, although he was more mentally taxing than physically threatening, I supposed.

Still, he wasn't wrong.

"I'll be safer," I promised him.

"See that you are," he said.

Then he helped me clean up the remains of lunch and quench the fire. The sun was past the halfway point from noon to sunset when we parted ways, and I hurried my steps back to the cabin.

I had left Mjolner there with my grandmother, which normally would be protection enough. But Mjolner wasn't going to be much of a defense against Odd's too-sharp tongue.

And even my mild-tempered grandmother had her limits.

CHAPTER FOUR

By the time I reached Frór's cabin, the sun was already setting behind me. The wind was picking up, cold but also treacherous. The sky above was still largely cloud-free, but the air was filled with a chilly mist from the lake.

I crossed the narrow part of the promontory slowly and with great care, grateful for my walking stick. I was wearing my winter hiking boots, their treads almost cleat-like with their ability to hold on to the ground beneath me. So far as I knew, no one had ever fallen from this road, not even in the harshest gale.

But there was always a first time.

After I reached the far side and the road once more had stretches of meadow grass on either side of it, I relaxed and picked up my pace. It was already too late to head down to the shore for my nightly texts with Andrew. I had spent too long ambling through the forest around my cottage instead of heading straight back to the cabin. I told myself I was taking a walking meditation, letting Haraldr's lesson sink into my mind in a more passive way before I started the real work of communing with the rune.

But as my steps slowed more and more as I approached the cabin's door, I had to admit to myself that mostly I was just dreading being back in Odd's company.

I opened the cabin door and was at once blasted by a wave of warm air and the smell of roasted meat and potatoes and baking bread. My grandmother and I had been keeping our meals pretty simple since we'd come out to the cabin, mostly a variety of soups we took turns concocting. But apparently the arrival of Odd had prompted my grandmother to go full out.

Maybe there *was* an upside to his visit. My mouth was already watering, and I still had to get my jacket and boots off.

Mjolner appeared at the edge of the step up out of the mudroom to the great room. He just blinked, but I knew what he meant. He didn't like the intruder.

"I know," I told him, giving him a scritch around the ears. "Surely you can hide in my room?"

Since he could walk through walls and apparently even teleport over great distances, he could escape to anywhere he liked. My bedroom in Villmark, or in Runde, or I suspected even to where Frór or the Thors were, somewhere out in the wilds of the north.

But he just blinked again and gave me a small, indignant meow before turning away from me to dash up the steep stairs to the loft.

"Has he been like that all day?" I asked my grandmother as I came into the kitchen area.

"Hm? Oh, Mjolner? Yes, he's been letting me know he's not pleased," she said as she stirred at a pot of gravy. "Can you get the lingonberry jam out of the icebox? I think we're just about ready here."

"Our guest must be quite the big eater," I said as I surveyed the array of dishes already crowding the surface of our little table. "Either that, or the Thors are stopping by. All five of them."

"I had a craving," she said as she gently nudged the breadbasket to one side and the plate of roasted potatoes to the other to make room for the gravy.

"For what?" I asked as I fetched the jam.

"All of it?" she said and gave me an apologetic smile. "It's too much, I know. But neither of us will have to cook again for a week."

"I haven't seen a spread like this in years," Odd said from behind me. I turned to get my first look at him without his hat and cloak on.

He had two eyes, and neither of them were glowing. I didn't quite understand my own little stab of disappointment at that fact.

He had bathed and changed out of his mud-spattered clothes. His long silver hair was still damp and looked a little odd after being aggressively combed. His beard was combed smooth as well, but he had tucked it back into his belt.

It was a look.

If I had to guess, I would say he was my grandmother's age. But in all honesty, I don't exactly know how old she is either. His face was weather-beaten, his skin obviously sunburnt and frost-nipped many times over to a dark, leathery texture. But as he rolled up his tunic sleeves to dig into his food, I saw his forearms were still as thickly muscled as any youth's.

He filled up his plate with great heaping portions and ate with gusto. It was only after having seconds that he even started to chat with my grandmother.

This conversation was all about people they had known years ago, people I didn't know at all, and it was in a version of Villmarker Norse that I had to work to understand.

So I quietly excused myself and washed up my plate before heading to my easel in the far corner of the room. I clipped the rune card Haraldr had given to me to the top of the easel and dug out a stick of charcoal.

I always seem to get into the flow faster with charcoal than with pencils. Maybe it was the way I got my whole hand into it, rubbing and blending with the heel of my hand or my fingertips.

I had expected this new rune to be tricky for me to connect with, but I quickly found the opposite to be true. It was like I could feel a wind blowing through me, the breath of inspiration.

Haraldr had been right. This *did* feel like it came from the same place as my own art.

"What nonsense is this?" Odd asked from over my shoulder. I

hadn't even sensed him approaching, and his voice so close to my ear made me jump. Again.

And completely shattered my flow.

"Nothing," I said, trying to cover my work with my hands. But I was using my largest size of paper, and I had filled the page already with overlapping Ases.

"I know this," Odd said, snatching the card from where it was clipped to my easel. He frowned at it as if he found it difficult to see by the firelight. "Ase. Ansuz. Óss." Then he closed his eyes and hummed to himself for a moment. When he spoke again, his voice was deeper than before, reverberating through the entire cabin. "Óss er algingautr ok ásgarðs jöfurr, ok valhallar vísi."

It took a moment for the last rumblings of his voice to finish echoing around the room. Then he opened first one eye and then the other to look at me. "I suppose you know that one?"

"No," I admitted. I wasn't even sure I could tell what language he was speaking. It wasn't Norwegian, nor quite Villmarker Norse, either. But it was close. I knew he had said something about Asgard and Valhalla for sure, but the rest was lost to me.

"What you're doing is of no use," he said, tossing the card back at me disdainfully. "How can anyone hope to master the runes if you don't even know the runic poems? Useless."

"I have my own ways," I said. I realized I was crumbling the charcoal stick I was clenching too tightly in my fingers and deliberately set the remains aside.

Odd just turned back to fix that eye on me. No, both eyes. I don't know why I kept thinking he was using only one. I could see them both looking at me now. Neither was glass or anything.

The question of the number of his eyes aside, the meaning in that glare was clear.

Half-literate misinterpreter of runes.

Only now I suspected the "half-literate" was being downgraded to "illiterate."

"Learn the poems. Learn the words. Their meanings are in their sounds. Sounds are controlled air. That is how they have meaning. This," he said, sweeping a hand over my easel and supplies and finished work stacked against the wall all, "this has no air. How can it? So it's nothing."

Then he turned to where my grandmother was standing as if frozen in place, halfway through filling a storage container with the remains of the roast. "I'm going for a walk," he told her, then tromped into the mudroom and quickly out the door.

I looked back at my page of charcoaled runes. A moment before, I had felt so connected, with that rune and through that rune to all the deeper things my magic was based on.

Now? Now, they looked like childish scribbles. A child copying the shapes of letters she doesn't yet know how to read.

"Ingrid. Come help me put this food away," my grandmother said.

I went to the sink first to wash the dark dust from my hands, then took out another lidded container to transfer the peas and onions out of the serving dish.

"It was a lovely dinner, mormor," I said, by force of will keeping my voice from shaking.

"Wasted on bad company, I think," she said with a scowl.

I looked up at her, startled. "Did he say something to you?" I asked. I had completely tuned out the end of their conversation, but I could see she was quite upset.

"I heard what he said to *you*," she said, slamming mashed potatoes off her spoon with too much force.

"Should I let it bother me?" I asked. "I mean, does he know what he's talking about? If he's as old as he says he is, he must know a lot of things. Like the rune poems, for instance."

"Haraldr can give you as many books of poetry as you could ever wish to read," she said, still slamming spoonful after spoonful of potatoes into the container. Then she clapped the lid on top of it and forced it down. There were too many potatoes for that bowl. They squished out all over, but she didn't even seem to notice.

"But he never gave me any," I said.

"Perhaps because he knows best what you need to learn," she said. She stood with her hands on her hips, her breath seething in and out of her, and I could feel a prickling all over my skin. Like static electricity just waiting for me to touch something to give me one hell of a zap.

"Mormor?" I said.

She looked up at me and in an instant she was calm.

Then she noticed the mess with the potatoes.

"Every time," she said, shaking her head with a little laugh. "He does this to me every time."

"And here I thought it was just Frór who rubbed you the wrong way," I said.

"Yes, well. That's different," she said, then went to fetch a paper towel to clean up the sides of the potato container.

"I think you should tell me more about this Odd fellow," I said, stacking the peas and onions container on top of the meat and the gravy containers and bringing them all to the icebox.

"He'll be back soon," my grandmother said in a low voice, glancing over her shoulder towards the door. "Look, I don't know if he's as old as he says he is. He's older than me, and that's plenty old enough."

"Surely there's some sort of record?" I said. Although I had never seen it, I knew the council kept something called the Book of the Settlement with all the names of all the Villmarkers recorded.

"Well, that's just it," she said, licking a dollop of potato off her finger before handing me the container. "He says his name is Odd Oddsen, but that's clearly fake. We've had several Odds in Villmark over the centuries, but no Odd Oddsens. Not even among the first settlers."

"So he's lying," I said. "Why doesn't anyone call him on it?"

"He just spins more tales. He always has an answer, and when you find the answer doesn't quite fit the truth as we know it, he spins another. It's endless. And anyway, he never sticks around long enough for anyone to dig terribly deep into any of it."

"But he's a troublemaker?" I guessed.

"He stirs things up," she said. "If we're lucky, he'll only torment the two of us out here at the cabin and not go into town at all. If we're all very, very lucky."

"Why? What are you afraid will happen?" I asked.

She looked over her shoulder at the door again before stepping closer to me. "You know that Villmark has become divided, and those divisions are growing. Slowly, but growing."

"The isolationists," I said.

"Exactly," she said. "There have always been those who want closer relations with the outside world, and those who want nothing to do with it. But the more different the two worlds become, the harder it is for those two groups to get along. And every time Odd is in town, things get worse."

"So he's a rabble-rouser?" I asked.

"I've never heard him make a speech or anything like that," she said. "It's more like his mere presence makes people restless."

"I'm not disagreeing with you at all, but I find it hard to reconcile," I said. "Every time I look at him, I'm put in mind of Odin."

"Oh, he does that on purpose," my grandmother said with a laugh. "Always has. He has a magic I don't understand, but I can feel it. It's different from ours."

"More powerful?" I asked.

She just shrugged. But she didn't look happy.

"In the myths, Odin liked to travel the world of humans and visit them without ever dwelling among them," I said slowly. "Is it possible he *is* Odin? Or a manifestation of his power or something? I mean, a year ago, I didn't even think magic was real. Where do I draw the line? Before or after 'the old gods are real'?"

"I can't answer that question for you," she said. "I *can* tell you that I think it's all true in our minds. Not that it's make-believe. Nothing is true except for what's in our minds."

"I don't follow that at all," I admitted.

She gave me a tired smile. "It's the kind of thing you understand through experience, not through words. But let me try again. We all experience this world together, but we experience it individually, through our own minds. Sometimes our minds agree on something, and other times they don't. I look at Odd, and I don't see Odin. Not at all. But others in Villmark have before and surely will again. Am I right and they're wrong? How can I say? I can't see the world through their eyes. And such things can't be proven."

"So if everyone who believes he's Odin does what he says, even if it's really bad stuff, we just allow it because we can't know or prove he isn't Odin?" I asked, shaking my head. What a dark world that would be.

"No, not at all," she said cheerily. "Bad ideas are bad ideas. It doesn't matter where they come from. We can argue against those courses of actions on their merits."

"I suppose so," I said. But I didn't find that very comforting.

"Look," she said, taking my arms and looking me in the eye. "Odin, like all of our gods, is there to guide and inspire, not to be worshiped. That's not how our people do things. So even if you decide that Odd really is a living manifestation of the Odin power, that doesn't mean you have to agree to do anything he says. Defying the gods is what we humans do."

I wanted to laugh. Her words had the cadence of a joke. But I couldn't do it. It was all just too overwhelming.

"I hope you're right and he leaves soon and never goes into town," I said. "In the meantime, I think I'm heading to bed before he gets back from his little walk."

"Keep Mjolner with you," she said. I gave her a quizzical look, but she just smiled at me. "Your first night after beginning with a new rune tends to give you powerful dreams, right? Keep Mjolner close. He'll guard your sleep."

"I will. Good night, mormor," I said.

"Good night," she said.

I left her in the kitchen making herself one last cup of tea. I peeked into the open door of the guest room, but my half-formed hopes were quickly dashed when I saw the travel pack still sitting against the wall, its contents strewn about the room.

It would've been nice if his walk after dinner had been a walk away, never to return. But surely he wouldn't linger more than a day or two.

I climbed into bed, pushing Mjolner off to one side of my pillow so there was room for my own head, and quickly fell asleep.

CHAPTER FIVE

IF I DREAMED about the Ase rune or anything else, I had no memory of it. I woke to the smell of bacon and the sound of pans rattling around in the kitchen louder than the murmur of voices.

Voices. Plural. Odd was still with us.

Mjolner stretched and yawned, pushing at the back of my head with his six-toed paws. Clearly, he wanted me out of his bed. I got up and got dressed, made a stab at brushing out my red curls, then gave up when the growing static electricity made that almost painful. I opted to smash a beanie over it instead and headed downstairs.

My grandmother and Odd were both sitting at the breakfast table. Odd was alternating shoveling food in his mouth with pontificating on something. His ancient Villmarker Norse accent was so thick it was easy to tune him out as I ate scrambled eggs on toast at the kitchen counter, then took a cup of coffee to my easel.

My grandmother looked up at me as I brushed past her, and she gave me an encouraging smile, as if I were the one stuck there listening to this man go on and on. I gave her shoulder a little squeeze of solidarity.

I had never been so happy to have work to do.

I tore away the page from the day before and started fresh, this time with graphite pencils. Sometimes the slow connection was the strongest connection. I wasn't so much writing the rune as a letter as using the suggestion of its shape to sketch out little scenes. Flags in the wind. Sails of a ship. Bloomers on a laundry line. I don't know where that last one came from, but it had me smiling.

It felt like I had been sketching for hours, but it couldn't have been too long because when the sudden crash startled me back into the present, my grandmother and Odd were still in the kitchen with the remains of breakfast on the table between them.

"What happened?" I asked, searching for any sign of what had just gotten smashed.

"Nothing, dear. It's quite all right," my grandmother said. But the smile she was giving me was as tight as a high tension wire.

"What made that crash?" I persisted, pushing away from the easel and getting to my feet.

"It's fine, dear. Why don't you take a walk? That always helps you get into the flow, doesn't it?"

Ironic. I had just been in the flow before their argument or whatever. I looked at Odd, but he was just gazing at me steadily. With one or two eyes; I don't know anymore. If he felt guilty for anything, or was stewing in anger, or had any feelings at all, I couldn't tell.

"Bring your sketchbook with you." My grandmother's voice was still tight, but her eyes were pleading.

"Mjolner is just upstairs," I said. I wondered if Odd had even met my cat yet. It seemed like Mjolner had made himself scarce since Odd had arrived, hanging mostly in my bedroom despite the better sunbathing being in the window-seats downstairs.

"Thank you, Ingrid," my grandmother said, and bent to pick up the remains of a coffee mug from where they had fallen after being smashed against the wall behind Odd's head.

She was *so* telling me later what that was all about. But she clearly wanted me out of the house for a while. I put on my boots and jacket, slung my art bag across my body, and reached for my trusty walking stick.

The minute I stepped outside, I was lashed in the face by a freezing rain. How long had this been going on? No wonder Mjolner had opted for a day in bed. There was no sun to be seen anywhere in the sky.

I pulled my hood down low over my eyes and trudged towards the main road. It was a drenching rain, but thankfully with no wind. The narrow stretch of road didn't scare me any more than usual, and soon enough I was walking south towards the woods.

Most of the snow was already gone from the ground, washed away by the rain. That left nothing but the dead, brown grasses among the gray of trees and stone. But if it got much colder, this rain would turn to snow and cover everything back up again. Springtime on the North Shore.

I was just debating heading towards my cottage, as even walking under the protective cover of the trees was wet and miserable, when I heard the snap of a branch and instantly froze.

I expanded my magical senses even before I looked around with my normal eyes. And regretted that I had once again left my wand under my bed back at the cabin.

I sensed something to the east of me through the trees, off the path but moving parallel to it. It wasn't a magical creature like a troll or the woodwives I had met before. It didn't glow like my grandmother or me either. It was more like something that had been a victim of magic than a user of it.

"Who's there?" I called in Villmarker Norse.

"It's just me," someone answered. Then a green-hatted head poked out from around a tree trunk, followed by an arm giving me a little wave.

"Leifr?" I asked.

He came entirely into view and gave me a nod as he made his way towards me, hands in the pockets of his coat. It was a modern world parka, brand-new, a more olive shade of green than his knit cap. He had modern boots as well, and wind-proof hiking pants.

Despite everyone speaking about him as if he were a child, I knew he was about twenty. But to look at him, his age was hard to judge. He was shorter than average, and very thin. That stature made him seem childlike, and yet the hollowness to his cheeks made his face look old. Little tufts of blond hair jutted out from under his cap, as light as a toddler's, but his blue eyes had a haunted look that spoke of a great number of tough years.

Clearly, in Villmark, I couldn't tell anyone's age just by looking at them.

"You're Ingrid," he said as he stopped in front of me.

"I am," I said. "I hope I'm not disturbing your walk."

"Likewise," he said, his lips twisting into a grin that didn't touch his eyes.

"I mean, I've been told you prefer to be alone," I said.

"Mostly," he said. He scuffed at the rocky path with the toe of one boot. "I know you wanted to talk to me, though. Haraldr mentioned it."

"You prefer the woods to Signi's living room," I said.

This time when he smiled at me, it had a little warmth to it. "Yeah," he said. "If we can keep walking, that's even better."

"By all means," I said. "I was just having a wander, so any direction you want to go, just lead the way."

He nodded, then looked around before pointing to the east. I nodded, and we headed off together.

He clearly felt at ease in the woods, but I had been warned about the dangers there more than once. I double-checked my own magic to be sure I wasn't inadvertently glowing like a beacon, then kept up a low-level awareness of everything around us as we walked.

"You're doing magical stuff right now, aren't you?" Leifr asked, startling me.

"Just making sure I'm not drawing attention and that nothing can sneak up on us," I assured him. "You can tell?"

"Kind of," he said. "But mostly because it was like you were less aware for a minute there."

I remembered what Haraldr had said, and asked, "do you mind if I look at you a little more closely?"

"Just look?" he asked skeptically.

"Just look," I promised.

He nodded, and we stopped walking. He stood in front of me, shifting his weight from foot to foot subconsciously.

Of course, this would be easier with my wand, but Leifr wasn't resisting me, and I had all the time in the world to wait for my awareness to adjust.

At first I just sensed what I had sensed before. That magic had touched him but not come from him.

Then I noticed this wasn't a single kind of magic. There was an overlap of patterns, like he had walked through spells like cobwebs and they clung to him still, if only in tatters. Some were recent, I would swear more recent than his return to Villmark months before.

But others were old, older than any spell I had seen before.

"You've really been through something, haven't you?" I said as I blinked back into the normal world. He gave me a glum nod, and we resumed walking through the trees.

I could sense that he wanted to say something, but he kept changing his mind. I didn't know if he wasn't sure if he could trust me or if he just couldn't find the words to start.

But I didn't press. I just waited.

We were heading deeper into the woods, where there were fewer birch trees and more ancient evergreens. Their wide-spread branches kept off most of the rain, and there was still snow here under their canopy.

"I was nine when I got lost," he said suddenly, as if the words had finally just burst out of him. "My family was hunting mushrooms. I was supposed to stay close to my sister, but I was annoyed with her. She was always so bossy."

I bit my lip to keep from interrupting. I was afraid if I asked questions he would clam up, but this was a startling revelation. I had no idea he had family still in Villmark. So why then was he staying outside of the village in Signi's house?

"I don't know if it would do any good to know, but maybe you can do more magic on me and find out just what happened to me," he said.

"Don't you know?" I asked. "Do you have amnesia or..." I had no idea how to say "post-traumatic stress disorder," in Villmarker Norse.

But I didn't need to. He was already shaking his head. "No, I remember every minute of it. Or every minute I experienced of it."

"I'm afraid I don't understand you," I admitted.

He stopped walking again, turning to face me, but then immediately looking down at his own boots. Again, I waited for him to find the words.

"Haraldr has found my family in the Book of the Settlement," he said. "I disappeared a hundred and sixty years ago, thereabout. My sister has descendants that still live in town, but anyone I knew is dead and gone."

For several long minutes, I just gaped. I knew from his eyes he absolutely wasn't joking. But why had Haraldr not told me about this when we had been discussing Leifr before?

Villmark still lived with a lot of Viking traditions, but that wasn't because they were in the past. It was the twenty-first century there, the same as in Runde.

And yet I knew the land beyond the mountains to the north was called Old Norway by everyone. I assumed it was called that because of the trolls and giants and dwarves that lived there.

But it made total sense that time moved differently there.

Or did it? My head was spinning.

But Leifr just kept looking at me with those sad old eyes.

"I'm so sorry," I said. He gave me another glum nod. "So you remember being alone in the woods for a hundred and sixty years? But you only aged a decade or so."

"Yes, that's the trouble," he said. "That's what I was hoping you could use your magic to help me figure out. I've aged a decade, but a hundred and sixty years passed here."

"And your memories?" I asked.

"It felt like so much longer," he said. "Like, thousands of years."

"I'm so sorry," I said. Those words sounded lame to me, but I had no others. "I promise I'll do all I can for you, but I'm really not very good at magic yet. My grandmother has more skill than I do. Maybe you should talk to her."

"She's not well," Leifr said at once, and I realized that he had already asked at least one person about this before.

"She's doing better, and I think she could use a project," I said, linking my arm through his. "Come, we'll go back to the cabin and have a little lunch. Or a lot of lunch; we have a ton of leftovers. And we'll see what my grandmother thinks. You shouldn't feel like you're all alone with what happened to you. You are still a Villmarker, and all of Villmark stands with you."

"Thanks," he said. Then, with an exaggerated casual air, he asked, "will Loke be there?"

"Not today," I said. "Do you know Loke?"

"We haven't met," he said. "But he's another person I want to talk to about this. But he's hard to find, isn't he?"

"He is at that," I agreed. "He's promised me to stop by on Wednesdays, so if you don't track him down before then, come back for lunch then. But in the meantime, let's talk to my grandmother."

"All right," he said.

We were just at the crossroads when the warm glow that had been animating him all through the woods became cold apprehension once more.

"What is it?" I asked.

He was looking toward the northern road. Not up it to where it passed over the hills to the north, but at the exact spot where I had first met Odd.

"No one else is there, right?" he said. "Just you and Nora?"

"We do have a guest," I admitted. "Odd Oddsen."

His whole body stiffened at the name and he started backing away from me, hands thrusting deep into his pockets once more.

"Leifr?" I called.

"I'm sorry, I can't today," he said, taking quicker and quicker steps away from me.

"But you wanted to see my grandmother," I reminded him. "She's there now."

"I'll come back," he said, which I doubted. He must have sensed that, because he hurriedly added, "next Wednesday. When Loke is here. Make him wait for me, okay?"

"I'll do my best," I said, still a bit stunned by his rapid change in heart.

At least he hadn't asked me to make sure Odd was gone by Wednesday. I wasn't sure if that was in my power.

Making sure Loke was there was going to be tricky enough.

CHAPTER SIX

When I went inside the cabin, I found my grandmother alone in her customary window-seat, sipping cider and ignoring the book open on her lap. The rain was lashing at the window beside her, obscuring her view of the lake, but she didn't seem to mind.

In fact, she seemed in quite good spirits.

I couldn't see any sign of Odd. I had no doubt those two things were related.

"Is he gone?" I asked after I had hung my jacket across three hooks in the mudroom to dry.

"Just out for a walk," she said. But there was such a merry tone in her voice.

"Mormor, what did you do to him?" I asked.

"Nothing!" she said. "I just set him straight on a few things. He spends so much time in the deepest past he can access, it's no wonder he's not keeping up with how this world changes."

"Okay," I said slowly, not sure what all that meant, or how it involved smashing coffee mugs. "Do you mean literally in the deepest past? Because I have some questions about that. And about what happened to Leifr."

"Leifr?" my grandmother repeated.

"Signi's ward," I said.

"Right," my grandmother said, rubbing at her forehead. "That's all very involved. And not a conversation I want to risk being interrupted by the likes of our current houseguest."

"After he leaves, then," I said. "Well, it couldn't have been too much of an argument if he's still staying here."

"He'll be back," she promised me and turned back to the window, taking another sip of her cider.

I sat down at my easel and looked over my pencils, trying to decide where to begin. Mjolner slinked down the stairs to curl up around the toes of my fleece-lined chalet shoes and promptly fall back to sleep.

We had our coziness back. Even though a part of me knew that was all going to end at any minute when Odd came back from his wet walk, it was easy to let myself forget. The comfortable silence in the cabin was all the more golden for having been so recently disturbed.

I resumed my sketching from earlier, but as I drew, my drawings became more intricate. Denser scenes with more subtle details. I didn't quite know what I was drawing until I saw it form under my pencil.

I was trying to draw the wind, I realized. I was trying to draw breath. Not something blowing in the wind, or someone's breath fogging in cold air. I was trying to suggest the motion of air itself. Which, of course, can't be seen. So it was tricky.

Then I thought about how a picture is worth a thousand words. But what if that was too many? What if one word gave you one meaning, and it was the correct one, but a picture gave you one correct meaning and nine hundred ninety-nine wrong ones? How could you pick the single correct one out of all the wrong ones?

Then I decided I was thinking about it all backwards. The concepts behind the symbols had existed first. Then someone had written them down. Someone had *drawn* them as shapes.

That felt like a key to something, but I wasn't sure what. I was still trying to work out a way to repeat images in a motif, to try to make them rhyme in some way, when I realized my nose was almost pressed up to the page.

When had it gotten so dark?

I looked up to see my grandmother waking from a nap, stretching out her legs until her unread book fell to the floor with a bang. "Sorry," she said, bending to pick it up.

"No, I'm done for the day, I think," I said. "What time is it?"

"Past time for dinner, according to my stomach," she said, setting her book on top of the lap blanket on the window-seat and carrying her empty mug back to the kitchen. "What do you want to do with the leftovers? A little bit of everything?"

That would be easy enough to do with a microwave, but a lot of work without one.

"Cold meat sandwiches," I said at once.

"Perfect," she said, and opened the icebox, shifting the containers around in search of the roast.

I put my pencils away and brought my own mug into the kitchen. I set it in the sink, then turned to my grandmother. "He isn't back yet."

"I haven't seen him," she said.

"It's still raining out there. It'll probably turn to snow soon," I said.

"I know you probably want to go out looking for him, and I would agree that would be a good thing to do, except you and I both know he can go far too many places for us to search them all. I'm not even sure I can get to all of them in my current state," she said.

"You seem better," I said.

"I feel better," she assured me. "But I haven't tested myself yet. Not even a little."

"Are you scared to?" I asked.

"No," she said, too quickly.

She was scared. But I could hardly blame her for not wanting to face that fear for the sake of Odd.

"It's too dark to search," she told me as she started cutting last night's bread into thin slices.

We ate together in silence. Outside, I could hear the rain start to taper off. After rinsing my plate, I went to press my face to one of the windows. It looked like the rain had just stopped, not turned to snow as I had expected.

"I've had a bit of a day, so if you don't mind, I'm just going to take a cup of mint tea up to my room and read in bed for a bit," my grandmother said.

I smiled to myself, wondering how many times she was going to sit down with that book before she admitted it wasn't grabbing her. But maybe it was just an excuse to be left alone with her thoughts. Either way, I wasn't going to interfere.

"I'm going to walk down to the shore," I said suddenly. I don't think I had even formed that thought before the words were out of my mouth.

"Ingrid! It's after dark! That path is not safe," she said sternly.

"I'll bring my wand," I said. She scowled at me darkly, and I remembered too late it was Haraldr that had been nagging me about that. "And a flashlight," I added. She didn't relent. "I missed texting Andrew last night. If I miss twice in row, he's going to worry. Look, the rain's stopped."

"Wait for tomorrow," she said. "First thing in the morning, if you must."

"No, I feel like it has to be now," I said. She was still glowering at me, but I was distracted by something else. "Is it weird, like I feel like something is calling me?"

She continued glowering for a minute, but then her face softened as she closed her eyes. I watched as she reached out with her own senses. I could even feel her doing it, oh so tentatively. Like the first steps after a long time in a sickbed.

"I don't feel anything," she said when she at last opened her eyes, but she didn't look sure.

"I promise this isn't just about missing my friends," I said. "Although I do. A lot. I just feel like I need to get down to the shore."

"Did you feel this way when you were working before?" she asked, pointing towards the easel.

I thought about it. "No, I don't think so. It just hit me kind of suddenly, when you said you were going to bed. Although I don't think it was because of what you said. It felt like it came from outside."

"Go out, then," she said. The kettle behind her started to whistle, and she turned to fill her mug with the boiling water. "I'll be down here by the fire until you get back."

"I'm sure it's nothing," I said, but she was shaking her head before I even had the words out.

"You're sure of no such thing," she said firmly. "I wasn't called, so I'll wait here. Bring your wand, and your flashlight. And your cat, if he'll go."

"Right," I said, and ran up the stairs to my bedroom. I pulled out the box I kept my wand in and slid it into my art bag. Mjolner wasn't on my bed, but as I spun around to start searching for him, I saw him in the hallway, washing his ears with one over-sized paw as he waited.

"Right," I said again, and headed back to the stairs.

On the way past the guest room, I saw Odd's pack just as it was the day before, open and with the contents scattered across the foot of the bed and on the little table by the door. He hadn't gone, but he hadn't come back either.

I headed out the door, Mjolner close on my heels. The air outside was so cold the first breath felt like a punch to my lungs. I clicked on the flashlight and held it in my right hand, my walking stick in my left, as I made my way over the snowless grass towards the top of the path down to the lake shore.

Everything was soaked with rain and quickly freezing in place. The grass crackled like broken glass under my boots, and the muddy soil beneath was slick.

It took three times longer than usual to get down the many switchbacks of the path, and I always took that path slowly. I was moving so slowly my muscles had no chance to warm up. The wind off the lake cut through my wind-proof jacket as if it weren't there at all, and I thought longingly of where my grandmother was now, close to the fire under a blanket with hot tea in her hands.

What if I had imagined the whole thing? The way it had happened, where I had declared my intention and only later felt like I had been prompted, was weird and unsettling. *Had* I made a decision? It felt like I had. I wasn't being compelled by magic, I knew that for sure.

I had been compelled by magic once before, shortly after I arrived at Villmark. I had been trapped in the thrall of Halldis, the woman my grandmother had refused to make her apprentice volva. Mjolner had set me free, but I would never forget what it felt like, being trapped like that. That had been a feeling I never wanted to live through again, but if I did I would certainly know it.

Was it possible that out of boredom and loneliness, I had imagined a way to make things more interesting?

But I didn't need to make things up to disrupt the repetitive flow of days at the lake shore cabin. Odd had done that handily enough.

The sudden buzzing of my phone startled me so severely I stopped walking, planting my walking stick and leaning on it for support until the buzzing stopped.

I had a lot of messages. More than two days' worth. Of course, when I wasn't heard from after day one, day two had probably been more than usually stressful for Andrew.

Poor Andrew.

But I didn't pull my phone out of my pocket. Following my usual discipline, I continued down the rest of the path, turning around the bend in the shore to follow it to my favorite flat-topped rock.

But I never made it that far. Because the minute I came around the jutting southeastern corner of the promontory, I saw something hung up on the taller rocks closer to the mainland. A body.

A body wearing a tall, wide-brimmed hat and a long cloak that flapped in the wind.

CHAPTER SEVEN

ᚠ

THE CLOUDS OVERHEAD WERE DISPERSING, leaving more and more stars exposed. Even as I stood there motionless on the lake shore, two clouds parted and the moon burst out, lighting up the world around me in a silvery glow.

It hit the body like a spotlight, making the white hair under the dark hat glow like liquid silver. I could even see it glint off the white of one open eye.

It was Odd, that was without question. But how had he gotten there? Had he slipped and fallen from the narrow neck between the wider promontory and the mainland? He was directly below it. It made the most sense.

But it didn't feel true.

I wondered if my urge to go outside had coincided with his fall. Had he sent a magical cry for help that I had just barely heard?

Mjolner leaned his body up against the side of my leg, gently reminding me that he was there.

"I'm going to need help with this," I said to him. I would have to climb on top of those rocks to even reach Odd's body, and I knew I would never be able to get him down myself. "Can you go find Loke for me?"

Mjolner meowed and padded back the way we had come.

I watched that cloak flapping in the wind for another minute or two, then sat down on my favorite rock and pulled out my sketchbook. As miserably cold and wet as that rock was, I only felt it for an instant. Then I was too wrapped up in my drawing to even notice it.

I sketched furiously until I had filled the page and only then really looked at what I was drawing. It was like two overlapping images. The one with the darker, surer lines was what was there before me: Odd's body on the rocks.

But the second image was sketchier, the lines lighter, and a bit blurred. It was Odd at the moment he had fallen backwards from the road above. I could see one foot still on the road, but the other had stepped back over nothingness. For a split second, it looked like it must have been an accident.

But then I saw the arms reaching in from just off the page. Pushing him.

The lines were so sketchy I wasn't sure if it was one pair of arms or two, let alone have any clue who they might belong to.

I turned the page and tried to draw that scene again, but no more details would come to me.

But Odd had been murdered. I had no doubts about that.

I put my sketchbook and pencil away and adjusted my bag to rest across my back. Then I walked over to the rocks to try to find a way up to Odd's body.

The moon was shining wetly off the rocks, and I could tell that everything was icing over as the temperature continued to drop. But I was only climbing to a level just above my head. If I fell attempting it, I wouldn't bruise more than my ego.

I picked a place where two of the rocks nearby almost touched and wedged myself between them, climbing like a spider between the two until I was high enough to reach the top of the flatter of the two and pull myself up.

Odd's body was draped brokenly over three different rocks. Both of his legs were skewed away from his trunk in impossible positions.

He looked like a marionette that had been flung to the ground and left there.

I looked up towards the top of the promontory ninety or so feet above me. I could see where part of the road had sheered away, leaving new rock exposed. I suspected he hadn't been pushed off the cliff so much as pushed back to where the edge of the cliff was too weak to hold him. When it had crumbled beneath him, he had stumbled another step back into nothingness.

I closed my eyes and tried to will the mental image away. But it glued itself to my recurring fears of falling off that part of the road myself. Now I could see it as if it were happening to me. Even to the point where I could almost feel my own body breaking on the rocks I was sitting on now.

I took a deep, steadying breath. And then I took out my bronze wand. I waved it before my eyes until I was seeing the magical world.

Even in death, Odd's body glowed with power. That power felt old beyond anything I had seen before. I felt a sudden twinge of regret. What knowledge had he died with, never passing it on to others? He had certainly seemed to know the runes. If only he could've accepted my learning style, he might have been an invaluable teacher to me. As much as I loved learning from Haraldr, he had no magic himself. That was often a stumbling block between us.

What more might I have learned if Odd had been willing to teach me rather than mocking me?

Now I would never know. I regretted not trying harder to get along with him. But then I remembered my grandmother hadn't gotten along with him either, and she got along with nearly everybody. In all likelihood, Odd would never have wanted to hang around and be my mentor at all.

Still, that pang of regret remained.

I focused again on what I saw through my wand. All the magic was deep inside him, native to him. There was no sign of any spell acting on him from without. Not that I had expected there to be. Why use magic when a pair of strong arms will do?

I put my wand away and crawled closer to Odd's side. He had

fallen on his back, and his eyes were staring up into the starry sky. I gently brushed my hand over his face, closing his eyes. Then I tugged his hat down to cover his face in case it started to rain again.

Having nothing more to do for him, I jumped back down to the lake shore, then climbed the switchbacks up to the top of the promontory.

Then I hesitated. I should search the narrow neck for clues, but I really didn't want to go out there. Not now, not alone. If I fell, no one would know for hours. What would I see by moonlight, anyway? Nothing that I wouldn't see better in the morning when the sun was out.

I went into the cabin. My grandmother was still in her chair by the fire, but she got up when she heard me come in.

"What is it?" she asked as I took off my art bag and set it on the floor.

"Odd," I said. "He's dead."

She looked stricken, fumbling until she found the back of the chair behind her to lean on for support. "Are you sure?"

"I'm sure," I said.

"It doesn't seem possible," she said. "I didn't think I'd believed him about how long he'd lived. But on some level, I must have. I just assumed he would carry on living forever. I was sure he would outlive me."

"Maybe he would have. Maybe old age had no power to take him. Maybe he would've carried on living forever if he hadn't met a violent end," I said darkly.

"What happened?" she asked.

"He fell to the rocks on the lake shore. From where the promontory is narrowest just before it connects with the mainland," I said. "But I'm pretty sure he was pushed." I took out my sketchbook and showed her my drawing. She studied it carefully, even touching her fingertips to the pencil strokes.

"Any idea who?" she asked me.

"No," I said. "Who even knew he was here?"

But she didn't seem to hear me, lost in her own thoughts as she was. "We never even heard anyone approach the cabin," she said, looking past me at the closed door as if she could see through it to the road itself. "No sounds of an argument. Nothing."

I heard a soft meow and looked up to see Mjolner trotting down the stairs from the loft. He had something clutched in his mouth. At first I thought he was bringing me a mouse, but when he spat it out at my feet, I saw it was, in fact, a wad of grayish paper.

A note. I went over to the kitchen table to smooth it out. "It's from Loke," I told my grandmother. "He and Roarr will be here at dawn. They're bringing a cart to carry the body away in. A narrow one to navigate the path down to the shore. That's going to be tricky. Even a wheelbarrow might be too wide. Still, better than trying to carry him up by hand, I suppose."

"How much did you tell Loke in your note?" my grandmother asked sharply.

"I didn't send him a note," I admitted. Then I scanned what he had written to me again. "He certainly seems to have a good grasp on the situation. To be honest, I assumed Mjolner would just lead him back here."

"All the way from Villmark?" my grandmother said.

"Maybe I didn't think it through," I said. "This isn't the first time it's felt to me like Mjolner and Loke have their own way of communicating. Although I've never felt it so strongly."

"He's a remarkable cat," my grandmother allowed. "I don't think I'm going to get a bit of sleep tonight. Are you sure you and I can't bring the body up ourselves?"

"Quite sure," I said. I didn't like the idea of leaving him out, exposed to the elements, either. At least it had stopped raining.

"I think we can rely on Loke to be discrete," my grandmother said as she paced the cabin floor, and I realized we hadn't been thinking the same thing. I had been worried about the body being out in the rain, but that hadn't been on her mind at all.

"Mormor?" I asked.

"Roarr too," she said, still not hearing me. "Bringing a cart. A narrow cart. Yes, I think Loke understands."

"Understands what?" I asked.

She finally looked up at me, surprised by my confusion. "Ingrid, do you have any idea what will happen when people in Villmark learn that Odd is dead? And worse than that, murdered?"

"Nothing good," I guessed.

"No. We need to at least try to keep this quiet until we know more," she said.

"How?" I asked. "Like I said, no one even knew he was here, or so I thought. But someone pushed him off the cliff, so someone knew. And if someone knew, others will know."

"We will make the best use of all the time we have," she said.

There was that word again. Time. Ironically, the time to discuss it was definitely not now.

"Well, I'm putting some coffee on," my grandmother said with a yawn and headed for the coffeemaker. "Extra strength, I should think."

"I'll have some," I said, bringing my sketchbook over to my easel. I doubted a larger sheet of paper would reveal any more clues than the first drawing had shown, but I had to at least try.

It was going to be a very long night.

CHAPTER EIGHT

As soon as the first sign of lightening sky appeared in the east over the lake, I got back into my jacket and hat and headed out to meet Loke and Roarr at the crossroads.

The first sliver of the sun was edging up over the lake as I left the cabin behind me. It hit the narrow slivers of meadow around me like a crescendo, glinting off of every blade of brown grass that was now encased in ice from the prior day's rain.

It was like the whole world around me was crafted from blown glass. The sudden beauty of it almost brought a tear to my eye.

Of course, missing an entire night's sleep always made my emotions swing like crazy. And there were a lot of hours still remaining between me and bedtime.

I slowed my steps as I reached the narrow neck between the promontory and the mainland, the very place Odd had fallen.

But rather than feeling my usual apprehension, I found my strongest emotion was actually curiosity. I scanned the ground around the path for any sign of what had happened the day before.

That spot where he had fallen was incredibly apparent. The road there looked like a cookie with a bite taken out of it, a sizable chunk of its surface, simply not there anymore. There was enough room left to get the cart across when Loke and Roarr arrived, but just barely. There would certainly be no room to walk beside it.

But I could see no other clues in the predawn light. No sign of blood or torn clothing or even a boot print. I sat down on the icy road and sketched all the details, but this time nothing magical emerged. I put my sketchbook and pencils away and continued on through the blown glass world to the crossroads.

There was no sign yet of Loke, Roarr, or the cart. I leaned on my walking stick as I waited, looking at each blade of grass around me, and then at the ice-covered trees of the woods. There would be a lot of broken branches before everything melted, a downside to the momentary beauty.

A flicker of motion far off to the west caught my eye, and I squinted towards it, just making out the top of Leifr's green hat as he walked through the rolling hills.

On a sudden impulse, I took out my sketchbook and started drawing. It was awkward drawing like that, standing with my feet planted wide and holding the bottom edge of the book tightly against my stomach so I could draw with the other hand. But I only needed a quick, rough sketch.

It was weird. Every time I started to draw his hat—which was all I could see of him—it became just another part of the landscape around it. It was like he wasn't really there. Or that he was, but that he was an indistinguishable part of the world around him. Either way, I got no sense of what he was up to from my sketch.

I put my book away and went back to waiting.

The sun was fully over the horizon before I heard the creak of wheels over the frozen ground. Then Loke and Roarr emerged from the forest, pulling a small cart behind them. The cart was narrower than the two of them standing shoulder to shoulder as they pulled it along themselves. No ox this time. Maybe they *would* be able to guide it down that path to the lake shore. I hoped so. The only other way down to the shore that I knew of was an hour's walk to the north, and it wasn't much wider.

"Odd Oddsen is dead, eh?" Loke said as they drew up beside me then stopped pulling to rest for a moment. Then he gestured to the bed of the cart behind him. "We brought tarps, but it's probably best if we wait until dark to bring him into Villmark."

I gave him a relieved smile. "My grandmother is going to be so pleased you've already thought of that."

"Of course," he said, and Roarr also gave a solemn nod. Then Loke asked, "so, what happened anyway?"

"He fell from the road just up there," I said, pointing to the narrow neck.

"Not how I ever thought he would go," Loke said.

"How did you think he'd go?" Roarr asked.

Loke shrugged. "Fighting giants? I don't know. I just assumed when he died, it would be in some glorious moment. Not like this."

"He was pushed," I said. I showed them my sketch.

"Any idea by who?" Loke asked, touching the overlap of the arms at the edge of the page.

"No. I think it was just one person, but I'm not one hundred percent even about that," I admitted.

"But who even knew he was out here? He hasn't been in town at all," Loke said.

I had been turning the same question over in my mind all night. "My grandmother knew, of course," I said. "Odd went out for a walk and just never came back in. But she was with me the whole time."

"At least she's not a suspect this time," Loke said. "Or you. If the two of you were together, then she's your alibi, too."

"Thanks," I said. "Nice to know you don't think I'm a killer."

"I think when it comes to Odd, anyone could be the killer," Loke said. "He rubbed just about everyone the wrong way at some point."

"We knew he was here," Roarr pointed out.

"Did *you* tell anybody?" Loke asked.

"No," he said.

"Nor I."

"I told Haraldr," I said.

"I think we can be pretty sure those aren't his arms you drew," Loke said with a twinkle in his eye.

"I also told Leifr," I said, then looked westward to where I had seen him last. There was no sign of him now.

"Leifr is a scrawny little fellow. Those aren't his arms either," Loke said.

"He said he's never met you," I said.

"Not formally, but I've seen him around. From a distance. But close enough to know he doesn't have arms like that."

"I agree," Roarr said, but he sounded far away, as if lost in thought.

"You've seen him too?" I asked.

"Yeah, from a distance," he said absently. "Not a big fellow at all."

"We might be reading too much into how I drew those arms," I said. "I don't recall having any specific vision in my head about it. Maybe those are stylized. Like the thickness is more to demonstrate the strength of intent than actual muscle."

"You think Leifr pushed Odd off the road?" Loke asked.

"It wouldn't take much to do it," I said. "We should really build some kind of safety rail for that stretch of road."

"Are you saying Leifr is a crazed killer?" Roarr asked. "I mean, he's in Signi's care because of what happened to him. Does that make him a danger to others? Wouldn't she know? Wouldn't she keep him from wandering the countryside if he were?"

"No, I don't think anyone else is in danger. He's not like a serial killer or anything," I said.

"But?" Loke prompted me.

"I invited him to lunch yesterday so he could meet my grandmother, but the minute he heard that Odd was staying with us, his whole demeanor just changed. He had very strong negative feelings about Odd."

"Didn't we all?" Loke said, but his joke fell flat.

"Why did Leifer hate Odd?" Roarr asked.

"I don't know. But he did," I said. "And he's always walking around here, off in the distance. He was out there just a few minutes ago, wandering around. What if he saw Odd out alone at the narrow neck of the road? What if he saw an opportunity and just acted?"

"I don't think so," Loke said. "Look at how you drew Odd. He wasn't blindsided. Whoever pushed him did it while they were standing face to face."

"So?" I said.

"Odd may be older than time, but you'd never know it by looking at him. He's as heavily muscled as any of the Thors. I really think that narrows our list of suspects to just the biggest men in Villmark. Certainly not Leifr."

I looked down at my sketch. I had to agree with Loke. Leifr didn't feel like he was the one I had drawn. But who else had been out this far from Villmark? Hunting parties went south and west, but no one in Villmark went north save the Thors. Not if they could help it.

"Come on," I said, putting my book away. "Let's go down and get his body before the birds get to it. We can argue about suspects after we get his remains back to town."

We once again approached the cabin to find my grandmother waiting outside. She gave us a nod, then led the way down the narrow path to the lake shore.

The sun was growing warmer as it rose higher in the sky, and the ice was melting in constant drips all around us. It made the wheels slip from time to time, slowing down our progress even before we reached the gravelly shore, where the wheels didn't want to turn at all.

"We can carry him this far, the four of us," Loke said. "Let's just get the cart facing the right way round first."

"And get the wheels off the loose rock," Roarr agreed. There wasn't enough room for me to try to help, not that my help was needed. Roarr was a typical Villmarker male, tall and broad-shouldered. He basically looked like a football player who liked to do a little blacksmithing in his spare time.

Loke, on the other hand, looked like a poet from the Romantic school. But he was stronger than he looked, wiry and agile. He negotiated the trickier front end, moving it around in a semicircle while Roarr just held up the heavier backend.

That done, the four of us walked around the outthrust of rock to the southern side of the promontory.

Odd's body was just as I had left it, cloak fluttering in the wind, wide-brimmed hat resting over his face.

"He really is gone," Loke said, but he sounded like he still didn't believe it.

"I've never met him," Roarr said. "I saw him once when I was a boy when he came into town. Some of the older boys pointed him out to me. But I never met him." Then he gave Loke a sideways glance. "You speak like you knew him better."

"I've met him," Loke said.

Those words hung in the air for a moment, but he said nothing further. Roarr opened his mouth to speak, but my grandmother jumped in first. "Let's get this done, the sooner the better. That sun is no friend to our business today."

"Right," Roarr agreed. "I'll climb up and lower him down, if the three of you want to catch hold of him." Then he looked at me. "He looks a little... broken?"

"He's all in one piece," I said. "Your plan is fine."

Roarr hoisted himself up onto the rocks with an ease that left me a little embarrassed for my scrambling climb the night before. He took a moment to carefully wrap Odd's arms against his body with his cloak, tying the ends like a baby's swaddling. Then he slid him down to us feet first.

I know there were three of us sharing his weight, but he still felt far too light. He had been so solid when I had met him out on the road. Now already he felt like little more than bones.

We carried him around to the cart and laid him gently in the bed. His hat was still over his face, and none of us made a move to disturb it.

"You have tarps," my grandmother said at last. "Good. The council should know what's happened before the public gets word of it, as much as that's possible."

"Loke said much the same," Roarr said. "We were planning to cover him and wait for darkness to enter the village both."

"Good," my grandmother nodded.

"Do you really think his presence will stir up so much trouble?"

Roarr asked. "I'm not the only one who barely knows the name Odd Oddsen. I understand you elders might feel differently about him since you knew him But I gather it's the likes of Raggi you're worried about. Raggi and his friends. But they're mostly my age. None of us knew Odd well or even really heard him speak. Is he so dangerous?"

"Better safe than sorry," my grandmother said, then gestured for Roarr to start pulling the cart back up to the cabin. Loke followed behind, pushing on the back end.

My grandmother chewed her lip for a moment, but caught my sleeve before I could move to follow the others.

"Mormor?" I asked.

"I have a feeling. A bad feeling," she said to me, her voice a low whisper all but lost under the sound of the waves on the shore.

"You still expect trouble?" I asked.

"Don't you?" she asked.

I closed my eyes and tried to sense what she was feeling. But in the end when I opened my eyes, I just shook my head.

"I want to know who killed him, certainly," I said. "But I don't have bad feelings about the future that follows this. I think it's going to be okay."

"I hope you're right," she said, then turned to start the climb back up to the cabin.

I lingered alone on the shore for a moment, my eyes on a ship far out to sea. I knew it was the sea, and not the lake, by the sails. I could just make out a flag snapping from the top of the tallest mast, although the colors were a blur of blue and red. Could be an American flag, or a Norwegian one, or any of a dozen other countries that used those colors.

But this flag was a swallowtail shape, two tapered ends flapping in the wind in a way that immediately brought my most recent rune to mind.

I hadn't dreamt about it, but I had spent enough time meditating on it for the usual seeing it everywhere syndrome to set in. But what if it wasn't just making itself known to me visually?

What if I didn't share my grandmother's bad feeling because this rune of order was making me see order where it didn't exist? Was it making me think everything was going to be okay even though it wasn't?

There would be no end to that sort of second guessing, and I immediately tore my gaze away from that ship and jogged to catch up with the others.

Whether or not there was some pending crisis to be averted, I still had a murder to solve. It was time to get my head in the game.

CHAPTER NINE

ᚠ

ONCE ROARR and Loke had the cart back up on top of the promontory, they parked it beside the cabin, out of view from the road.

Apparently, my grandmother insisted that they have breakfast before continuing back to Villmark. Not that I was inclined to argue. I was starving myself.

An overloaded plate of eggs, bacon, and far too many waffles later, I was almost too logy to even head back out the door. My sleepless night wasn't helping either.

But I knew what I had to do. "Mormor, I'm going with them to take the body into town," I said.

"I know, dear," she said with a smile. "Just help me put a few concealing spells on that cart before you go. Tarps and darkness are all well and good, but we have a few better ways of keeping things out of sight, don't we?"

I knew exactly what she meant. The web of spells we had maintained over her mead hall had served all sorts of functions, from keeping the beer fresh to discouraging the more inebriated patrons from starting fights. But a lot of them had been just to keep the

Viking-era hall from being noticed in the middle of the drably modern town of Runde.

But I was nervous. We hadn't done any magic together since all our spells over the mead hall had failed. As much as my gut was always insisting that my grandmother was completely rested, we hadn't yet actually tested her recovery.

"No worries, Ingrid. Just remember your breathing," she told me as we took up positions on opposite ends of the cart. As if I was nervous about my own magic and not hers. But her confidence was infectious. And the spells were familiar. Even after so many weeks without working together, the movements as we passed energy back and forth to each other were still automatic.

It felt good to be doing magic with my grandmother again.

"That should do it," she said when we had finished. Then she signaled for me to help her draw the tarps over Odd's body. She hesitated a moment before covering his head, as if she wanted to pull that hat away and take one last look at him.

But then she changed her mind, tucking her end under his shoulder to keep the wind from pulling it free. I did the same on my side. The minute I stepped back, Mjolner darted out from the open door behind me and settled on the cart, curling up against the dead body as if it was just another sleeping human to be napped with.

"I guess he's coming along," Loke said.

"It will be late before I get back," I said to my grandmother.

"I'll be all right," she assured me. "You have your wand?"

I patted my art bag resting on my hip.

Roarr alone pulled the cart with Loke and I following behind, but only until we were past the narrow neck where Odd had fallen. Once we reached the crossroads, Loke took the other handle to help turn the laden cart to the south.

I fell into step beside them, but my eyes were on the hills around us, searching for any sign of a green hat. There was nothing but the browns of grass now divested of its icy coat and the darker grays of tree bark still wet from the rain.

"I've been thinking about our assumption of how many people

knew Odd was in the area," Roarr said as we plunged into the woods, leaving the open meadows behind.

"The three of us plus Nora and Leifr," Loke said.

"And Haraldr," I reminded him.

"But none of them feel like suspects, we agreed," Loke said.

I wanted to argue about Leifr again. His anger had been so sudden and so strong, that I didn't think him committing a crime of passion could be ruled out without at least getting his alibi first.

But Roarr had more to say. "It's just that, you and I were talking about him when we walked back into town," he said to Loke.

"So, you think the trees ratted us out?" Loke teased.

"No, I think someone else might have been here with us," Roarr said. His cheeks were reddening as if he knew already that Loke was going to dismiss him, but he pressed on anyway. "I felt like someone was watching us as we walked. I've been thinking about it all morning, and I'm sure we were being watched. I don't think I was imagining it. It's at least worth looking into."

"Looking into how?" Loke asked, but then waved off the question before Roarr could answer. "Never mind. We've all seen Leifr roaming this area since he returned home from wherever he was. He likes to walk around here all the time, but he takes care not to be seen except at a distance. It was probably him, and he already knew. So it's no problem."

"I don't agree," Roarr said.

"I met Leifr on the road not too far from here," I said. "He only came out because he wanted to talk to me."

But even as I said it, I had doubts. Not that it had probably been Leifr in the woods near the road, but that if it had been that, he would have remained hiding. I knew he wanted to talk to Loke even more than he had wanted to talk with me. Had the presence of Roarr been enough to keep him away?

"I don't disagree that it was most likely him," Roarr said with quiet indignation. "I disagree that there is nothing else to be ruled out."

"And now I'm back to those spying trees," Loke said.

"No, not the trees," Roarr said. "The patrols."

Loke chewed on that thought for a minute. "They don't go this far out."

"And you know that how? You're sure?" Roarr pressed.

"Only the Thors come this far out," Loke said.

"*We're* this far out," Roarr said, but Loke just scoffed.

"Look, this is a pointless argument," I said. "We have better ways of figuring out who might have been out here. Roarr, do you remember where you felt like you were being watched?"

"Precisely," he said. "It's just up ahead, where the road dips in and out of a hollow. There's a tree that's fallen over a dark gray boulder."

"I know the spot," I said. Loke just shrugged as if the entire conversation bored him now.

When we reached the hollow, Roarr and Loke both set the cart handles down. I sat down in the center of the road and took out my sketchbook and pencils. Mjolner, in the back of the cart, opened one eye to regard me, then resumed his nap.

I set to work, drawing the woods around us. I drew everything to the west first, because that was where the rock and fallen tree were. Then I drew the woods around the path to the north. Then the woods to the east, the lake appearing in spots where the bare overlapping branches were particularly sparse. Then I drew the path to the south and the woods around it.

Only when I was done with all four sketches, did I put my pencils away and finally look at what I had committed to paper.

The south and west sketches showed nothing of interest. But something appeared on the far right side of the eastern sketch, and the far left side of the northern sketch.

"What is that?" I asked, touching my fingertip to the forms that appeared to be leafy undergrowth or mossy rocks hidden among the trees. I looked into the woods around us now, but they weren't there.

"Are you drawing this wood in the summertime?" Roarr asked. "But the trees don't have leaves. Only those people-shaped things do."

"People-shaped?" I said, sitting back away from my sketchbook and squinting at the images.

They were people-shaped.

"I know what they are," Loke said.

Roarr and I both looked at him, but he said nothing more.

"Well, what are they?" I asked.

"Wyldemen," he said. Then added, "Well, that one to the north looks more like a wyldewoman, but you know what I mean."

I had no idea what he meant.

Loke sighed. "Does the name woodwose ring any bells?"

It did not. I squinted at the drawing again, and then something clicked in my head.

"Are you talking about the Green Man?" I asked. "I thought that was a Celtic thing."

"You should read more," Loke said. I shot him a glare, which maybe he didn't deserve. I was still pretty sore from Odd implying the same thing. On the other hand, it already felt like I was spending my entire waking life studying without everyone telling me I wasn't doing enough reading.

"The woodwoses or wyldmen or whatever live in the deepest parts of the forest, where civilized people seldom go," Roarr said. "So that's why you drew them with clothes of moss and leaves in their hair and all that. And they ride stags like horses and live in harmony with all the beasts of the forest. Am I missing anything?"

"Nearly every culture around the globe has a version of it," Loke said, speaking more gently now, less judgy. "The Celts had theirs. We have ours. Even you modern types have the Sasquatch."

"I don't think that's the same thing at all," I said. Then I looked at Roarr. "You've seen these before?"

"Never," he said. "I've just grown up on the stories."

"I've met them," Loke said. Yet again, waiting for him to continue speaking led only to another long, silent pause.

"Do they live around here?" I asked at last.

"No. And I've never seen them come so close. But that doesn't mean it doesn't happen," he said with a shrug.

"But they might have been here for reasons of their own, and they might have overheard the two of you talking about Odd," I said, looking at my sketches again. But there were no more clues to be found.

"They certainly aren't suspects," Loke said.

"I don't know," Roarr said. "In the stories, they aren't necessarily gentle spirits."

"No, but they are very close with Odd," Loke said.

"You mean Odin in his traveler guise?" I asked.

"I mean this fellow. Odd Oddsen. He stays in their village from time to time," Loke said.

"How do you *know* this?" Roarr asked, exasperated. He was speaking for both of us, but Loke just gave another careless shrug.

He did this sort of thing a lot, projecting his complete apathy to whatever discussion was at hand. But I was starting to suspect that the more he acted as if nothing mattered to him, the closer the conversation was getting to something he didn't want uncovered.

I studied his face carefully. I was clearly making him uncomfortable, but he didn't abandon his façade of being above it all. He even leaned back against the tree behind him, arms crossed, letting his eyes droop as if a nap were about to overtake him.

"You did say that anyone who knew Odd was a suspect," Roarr reminded him. "I took that to mean that anyone long in his company would rather see him gone, if not outright dead. So if he was much in the company of these wyldemen, maybe he finally wore out his welcome?"

"No," Loke said with a long-suffering sigh. Then he pushed away from the tree to reengage with the conversation. "Look, the wyldemen adored him. I just don't see that ever changing to murderous intent."

"Maybe they know something, though," I said, tapping their image on my sketch thoughtfully. "I don't draw things like this without it meaning that there's something I need to look into."

"I know," Loke said. He was rubbing tiredly at the back of his neck.

"You know where to find them," I said.

"I do," he admitted.

"Then you should take Ingrid there to talk with them," Roarr said. "I'll carry on with the cart until I am closer to the village. If you finish before dark, you can help me pull it into town. Otherwise, I can handle it on my own."

"Are you sure?" I asked. It was a pretty steep hill into town.

"Go," he said with a nod.

"Keep out of sight," I said as I put my things away in my bag and snugged it closer to my body.

"I'll take this off the road when I'm a little further south and the ground is more level," he said.

Mjolner lifted his head to look at me with both eyes. Then he winked at me.

"Mjolner will keep you company," I said. "If you need help, he can fetch it for you."

"I'll be glad to have him," Roarr said solemnly.

"I'm sure we'll be back by dark," Loke said, clapping him on the shoulder. Then we watched Roarr pull the cart by himself up out of the hollow. It was slower going than with two, but he managed it without too much trouble.

"You don't seem very eager to take me to the wyldemen," I said as Loke turned to face back the way we'd come, towards the north. "Are they dangerous?"

"To us? Probably not," he said. "But I have no idea why Odd was so fond of spending time in their village."

"Why? What's wrong with them?" I asked.

Loke just sighed again then started walking north at a fast pace. "You'll see when we get there. Honestly, the things you drag me into."

I wracked my brain for every tale of wild men or the Green Man or even Sasquatch that I knew, but I had no idea what had him so loath to go find them.

I was just glad he was only metaphorically dragging his feet. Physically, it was all I could do to keep up with him.

CHAPTER TEN

I HAD WALKED along the road north of Frór's cabin before, just exploring and looking for other views of the lake to draw. That was how I knew about the other path down to the lake shore. But most of the walk was through more meadows that ended at a cliff face that loomed far over the lake below.

Or ocean. The farther north we went, the stronger the salty, briny smell to the air grew. And the birds overhead were foreign to the North Shore.

Beyond the point where I had turned back from my earlier walks, the meadows ended in another forest of evergreens mixed with birch. But these trees felt older to me. Even just the air under their branches felt older.

"Do you know where we are?" I asked Loke.

He looked over at me with a half-smile that had a tinge of sadness to it. "Less and less every day," he said.

"I meant right now," I said.

"I know what you meant," he said. "It's not much further."

"But are we still in Minnesota, or is this Norway, or something else all together?" I asked.

"It's probably safest to bet on the last of those," Loke said.

"My ancestress Torfa created a pocket dimension to contain Vill-mark," I said. "She made it to stretch back to Old Norway."

"I think it's more the other way around," Loke said. "In order to protect Villmark, she had to pull a pocket over from Old Norway."

"So this sense I get, like the bottoms of the pocket are fraying away, is all wrong?" I asked.

He looked at me with surprise. "I was about to say yes, that's all wrong. But now that you mention it, that's a nice metaphor. Let's ignore how it doesn't technically work that way. Things feel frayed. Yes."

"And you say my grandmother is maddeningly vague," I said.

"I don't mean to frustrate you," he said with a startling depth of sincerity. "I'm just trying to get it all straight in my own mind. I'm thinking I want you to help me with something, but it won't do any good until I know exactly what help I need. Please be patient with me."

"Always," I said. "Is this about your sister?"

"No, she's doing well," he said. Then the sadness was back. "Actually, this is about me."

"Well, when you're ready for help, you should speak to me and my grandmother both," I said. "Aside from having way more experience in magic than me, she's known you longer. And she's given a lot of thought to what goes on around you. You might be surprised."

"Maybe not in a good way," he said. Then he gave me an apologetic smile. "Let's talk about something else while we walk, yes?"

"Sure," I agreed. But I came up with nothing. We walked in silence for a while before I finally had something. "So you've not yet met Leifr."

"Signi's ward? No," he said.

"That's funny, because he seems very fond of you," I said.

"Fond of me how?"

"I would swear it was hero worship," I said.

Loke laughed. "I'm no hero."

"Not to must of us," I jokingly agreed. "But he sees something in you. He and I talked about him coming to the cabin on a Wednesday just to be there to meet you when you came with the supplies."

"I can't imagine why. Honestly, I can't," Loke said. "Who would've even been talking to him about me? And in what context?"

"I think the only people he speaks to are Signi and occasionally Haraldr. Neither of them seems likely to be singing your praises," I said. "But that was why I was sure Roarr was right that it wasn't Leifr who overheard you on the forest road. Because if he had been that close to you, I'm sure he would've come out to talk to you like he did with me."

"Yeah? Maybe Roarr scared him off. He was a suspected killer, you know. More than once."

"Again, not something I see either Signi or Haraldr mentioning," I said.

"Well, once we get this all sorted, I'll be sure to be there on Wednesday to meet him. Now I'm curious myself," he said.

There was a rustle around us. At first I thought we'd startled a rabbit. Then I amended that to a family of rabbits. I was just amending it again to a tribe of rabbits who, for some reason, had us surrounded when I realized we had arrived.

We had left the road behind some time ago to make our way more westerly through the trees and had reached a clearing of sorts. Not a break in the trees, but a wooded hollow that was sparse of underbrush. I looked around and saw figure after figure emerging from behind trees and rocks. They were smallish people that I at first glance took to be part tree like the moss-wives who had saved me from the Wild Hunt.

But as they drew closer, I saw they were men and women both, and while they were covered with moss and dried leaves, these were serving as clothing and not part of their bodies.

They had a stooped sort of walk as they drew closer to us, but their wide smiles were very friendly. I felt one of them slip their hand in mine, and another did the same to Loke. They drew us deeper into the hollow until we too were stooping to get under the branches of a large, thick evergreen tree.

A dozen or so wyldemen and -women were gathered inside. The moment they caught sight of us, they started thrusting plates of food at us. The plates were crafted of thick slabs of bark, and the food this late in the winter—or rather early in the spring—was meager indeed. Sad little lumps of forest berries and dried bits of rabbit jerky.

But the tea in wooden cups was surprisingly good. I had no idea what it was made out of. Something like lemongrass, but with floral notes I couldn't quite identify. I guessed that showed on my face when I took my first sip, because they all grinned at me as I took a second, larger gulp.

But even as Loke and I sat in their company and ate as sparingly as we could and still be polite, I knew at once why Loke hadn't been exactly thrilled to come.

Because as much as they were all friendly and clearly took hospitality extremely seriously, not a word they said made any kind of sense. It wasn't just a language that I didn't understand. It didn't sound like a language at all. It was like the babble of a child.

And it was a lot of babble. So, so much. Everyone had something to say, and they were saying it all at once, and none of it seemed like it meant anything.

I would've thought people who had remained hidden in the woods for millennia would be quieter. In fairness, none of them had said a word until we were safely under the tree. But Loke already looked worn out, rubbing at his forehead as two of them chattered at him at once.

Then, to my complete surprise, Loke babbled back at them.

"You understand them?" I asked.

"As much as they can be understood," he said. "Most of what they say is just happy sounds. They just like to hear the sounds they make, like vocalized singing without lyrics."

"But you can follow it?" I asked. Loke just shrugged, but I was distracted by a shift in the mood around us. The happy sounds, as Loke called them, were changing into something more melancholic. There was no wailing or crying, and yet I knew they were mourning something.

Or rather, someone.

"You told them about Odd?" I guessed.

"Yes," Loke said. "They were fond of him, like I said. He was their most frequent guest."

"Odd teach words me," a wyldeman said to me, too close and too loud. I just barely resisted the urge to flinch away.

"Did he?" I asked, hoping my modulated tone would serve as an example.

But it did not.

"He did!" the wyldeman said proudly. "He teach words me again. More words. More again."

"I don't think so, I'm afraid," I said. "He's gone now. Dead. You know that word? Dead?"

"I know dead," he said. "Odd dead. Odd dead again. Odd dead again again."

Now I was the one rubbing at my head. Loke just grinned at me, happy to share the growing headache.

"See what I mean? It almost makes sense," he said.

"Maybe I'm saying it wrong," I said.

"No, he understands you," Loke said. Then he turned to the wyldeman who was still grinning proudly at me. "Odd is dead. Pushed off a cliff. His body was left to the birds."

"Bad thing," the wyldeman said with a sad shake of his head. "Bad thing, that. Odd good man. Good Odd. Odd dead."

"Yes," Loke said.

"Odd dead dead again again," he said.

"I feel like he means something with that," I said to Loke. "Do they believe in reincarnation? Because it sounds like he means that."

"Oh, who knows?" Loke said impatiently. "Some of you were south. Some of you were watching me."

"Some hear things you," the wyldeman said. "We talk. We we talk talk. We hear you and talk talk."

"And what did you all decide?" Loke asked.

"Odd dead dead again again," he said.

"Would this go better in their language?" I asked.

"All their language is like this," he said with a sigh. Then he said to the wyldeman, "when was Odd here last with all of you?"

The wyldeman rolled his eyes up and touched the tip of his tongue to his teeth as if they were some sort of abacus. "Day day day day," he said with confidence.

"Is that the last time you saw him?" Loke asked.

"See him now," the wyldeman said, and spread his hands to encompass the world all around us. Or maybe just the tree. It wasn't clear.

"Look," I said, and dug my sketchbook out of my bag. "I'm a volva. Do you know what that means?"

Everyone under the tree oohed at once, a slow gasp of awe. Their eyes were wide and every pair of them were turned reverently towards me. Not since I had sat in judgment before an audience of trolls had I seen such adoration.

Clearly, in just three words, I had completely oversold myself.

"Just show them the sketch," Loke said, a hand over his mouth not quite concealing his smile.

"Right," I said, and turned the open page of the book towards the wyldemen. "This is Odd, here," I said, tapping the page. Then I tapped the arms. "Do you know who this might be?"

"Bad man," the wyldeman said with a fierce scowl. His hand was groping the ground beside him as if reaching for his spear.

"Did you see the bad man?" I asked.

"Bad man. See bad man, kill bad man," he said.

"You killed him?" I asked.

"I think he's speaking hypothetically," Loke said. "If they see him, they'll kill him."

"Then they know who he is?" I asked.

Loke gave a humorless laugh. "No. Best we keep the Villmarkers out of the woods for a bit, yeah?"

"So we've just made things worse?" I asked, my heart sinking into my stomach. I let the sketchbook slide off my lap, and the wyldeman snatched it up to turn the pages. The others gathered close around him to look over his shoulders.

I sank into a reverie, trying to figure out what I could do next. The wyldeman kept turning the pages, and there was an occasional murmur from the crowd at something they liked or recognized. I was tuning it all out until they all cried out at once.

"What is it?" I asked, reaching for my sketchbook.

"Boy man boy," the wyldeman said, and showed me the page I had drawn that morning of the meadows west of the crossroads.

The page where I had attempted to draw Leifr.

"You can see him?" I asked. I swept my gaze over the entire sketch, but I could still see not a single detail that indicated Leifr to me.

"Boy man," the wyldeman insisted. He jabbed a finger at the page, but it never landed on the same spot twice.

"Leifr?" I asked.

"Leifr boy man," the wyldeman agreed, nodding. "We help boy man. Odd say word no. No help boy man. Boy man lost. We help boy man. Odd say word no. We help help."

"Okay," I said, not sure what any of that meant. Besides that they knew who Leifr was.

And it sounded a lot like Odd told them not to help Leifr when he was lost. Which would explain why Leifr hated him so intensely.

But why would Odd tell the wyldemen not to help a lost little boy? I had found him personally abrasive, and so had my grandmother. But there was a huge leap from that to leaving a lost little boy alone in the woods to die.

"Loke?" I asked.

"I don't understand it any better than you do," he admitted. "But I don't think we should wait until Wednesday to talk to Leifr."

"No, I agree," I said.

As much as I thought we must be closer to Old Norway this far north, the wyldemen had pretty much perfected the Minnesota good-bye. It took nearly an hour to get out from under that tree, and we only managed it after I had accepted an entire cloth sack full of their particular kind of tea. But then Loke and I were on our way, heading back towards the south, and specifically towards the hamlet in the woods outside of Villmark where Signi lived with the other Villmarkers who had left home to try life outside the pocket dimension then returned again.

Conversation with Leifr would have its own challenges, but no way would it be harder to understand than our talk with the wyldemen.

"You believe me now?" Loke asked as we reached the road out of the woods and picked up speed.

"I believed you before," I said. "I understand you now. Are you going to tell me how you came to learn their language?"

"Not just now," he said. "It's going to be tight getting to Leifr and then to Roarr before dark."

I couldn't disagree with that. Unfortunately, even walking at a pace too strenuous to allow for talking didn't slow the running of my thoughts.

Just what had Odd been up to? And who wanted him dead?

As fast as we were moving, it didn't feel like we were getting any closer to that.

CHAPTER ELEVEN

Just being inside of Signi's house had a calming effect on my mind. All the cheery light, the brightness of the fabrics and the whiteness of the furniture, and above the all preponderance of books just put me at ease. The fire burning in her fireplace smelled of roasted apples, and after a day spent walking in the cold wet, its dry warmth on my cheeks was divine.

"You might want to go easy on that tea," Loke said. I had been squatting close to that fire to warm my hands, and I looked back over my shoulder to where he sat slumped in one of her white chairs. He looked terribly out of place, like a goth kid at a princess party.

"She hasn't brought the tea yet," I said.

"I meant what the wyldemen gave you," he said, nodding towards my art bag. "You drank a lot of it back under the tree."

"I'm sure if there was anything intoxicating in it, the walk here worked it all out of my system," I said.

"Suit yourself," he said with a maddening smile.

I moved away from the fire to sit in the chair next to his. Was I under the influence of something? I felt warm and content, but that was just from being indoors.

"Earl Grey all right?" Signi called from the kitchen.

"Perfect," I said, ignoring Loke's smirk.

Then she appeared in the doorway, a look of concern on her face. She matched her home, dressed in white but cozily so in warm wool leggings and a knee-length sweater that looked as soft as a cloud. I was a little worried at that look on her face and what it portended, but then she said, "too late in the day for caffeine?"

"Not for me," I assured her. "I was up all night, and I don't know when I'll be going to bed tonight."

I looked over at Loke in case he had opinions about late afternoon caffeine. His eyes were still laughing at me, but he just shrugged.

"If you're sure," Signi said, and disappeared into the kitchen again.

"You drank that tea too," I hissed at Loke.

"I pretended," he said. "Come on, Ingy. I'm always like this. But you, right now, are downright giddy."

"Inappropriate?" I asked, pressing my hands to my face as if I could change my mood by manually adjusting my facial expression.

"I think you'll be fine. None of us were Odd fans here," he said.

"No, that's true enough," Signi said as she came into the room with a laden tray. I moved things from the low table so that she could set it down. She sat on the edge of her own chair before pouring out the tea. I reached for mine at once, but it was too hot to take more than the smallest of sips.

Loke made sure he had my attention before deliberately faking a sip.

Whatever he said, he was in a strange mood too.

I was going to have to toss that tea when I got home. Which was a shame. It had been really tasty.

"Leifr will be down in a moment," Signi said as she sipped at her own tea. "I wanted to talk to you a bit first."

"We don't want to upset him or interfere with his treatment in any way," I assured her. "We just hope he might know something. The wyldemen were hard to understand, but they seemed to know him."

"Yes, from what you said, it sounded like Odd commanded them not to help Leifr, which seems so strange," she said with a frown.

"Do you believe him? About how much time passed?" I asked her.

Out of the corner of my eye I could see Loke raising an eyebrow at me, and I realized I hadn't tried to talk to him about that.

"I believe that he believes it," she said, setting her cup and saucer down. "Honestly, I don't know what to make out of it in any larger sense. I left Villmark as a teenager to study in the greater world, and even before then, I had little interest in anything magical."

"But Haraldr found his parents' names in the Book of the Settlement," I said.

"He did," Signi agreed, then sighed. "I agree, the most logical explanation is that he is telling the truth. Assuming that it is possible." She gave me a questioning look.

"I'm still learning, but I'd say yes, it is," I said.

"Can you fill me in?" Loke asked. "How old is Leifr?"

"He's either our age, or he's a hundred and seventy, or he's thousands of years old," I said.

"Thousands?" Signi asked, surprised.

"He didn't tell you?" I asked. "That's what it felt like for him, apparently. Thousands of years. And I don't think he meant that metaphorically or anything."

"No, he didn't tell me," Signi said sadly. "Poor boy."

"The wyldemen would leave me things," Leifr said from where he was standing at the bottom of the stairs. "When I was hungry, especially, they would leave me food. More when I was younger, or when the winters were bad."

"Thousands of winters?" Loke asked blithely.

"Thousands," Leifr confirmed. But his eyes were bright as he came into the room to sit on the chair next to Signi's. He was practically glowing, so excited to see Loke.

"You saw the wyldemen?" Loke asked.

"Not as such," Leifr said. "They never came out to talk to me or anything like that. Never face to face. But I would find things, and one of them at least would be sure I saw them before they all disappeared again."

"If they didn't try talking to you, believe me, they were doing you a favor," Loke said.

I thought the joke a little inappropriate. Leifr had been alone for thousands of years. Maybe no joke was appropriate.

But Leifr didn't seem to mind. If anything, he looked honored to take a little ribbing from Loke.

"How do you know Loke?" I asked.

But Loke waved the question away, leaning forward to ask instead, "how did you know Odd?"

"Odd Oddsen," Leifr said, and his expression darkened to an alarming shade of purple. Signi rested her hand on his knee, and he calmed a little.

But only a little.

"The wyldemen knew him," I said.

"Yes. They scatter when he commands it," Leifr said. "When he was near, I went hungry. No gifts from the wyldemen until he moved on. Even when I was little."

"Did you ever meet Odd yourself? Face to face?" I asked.

"On occasion," Leifr said. His hands on his thighs were in tight fists, pressed together as if his wrists were bound. And he wouldn't meet my eyes, just kept staring down at his hands like that.

"Odd wouldn't help you," Loke guessed.

"Never," Leifr spat out.

"I know it," Loke said. I gave him a questioning look, but he, too, wasn't making eye contact with me.

"Is it hard remembering events in sequence?" he asked Leifr.

"Not really," Leifr said. "My early days are only impressions now, but I remember the last few hundred years well enough."

Signi sucked in a breath but said nothing. I could sense how badly she wanted to get up and run for her notebook, but she didn't want to break the moment.

"Do you know who wanted Odd dead?" I asked.

"Who didn't? Who wouldn't?" he said with a laugh that touched on hysteria.

But when Loke said, "just recently,", Leifr calmed at once. His hands even loosened up until he was resting his palms on his thighs.

"Recently," he said as he scanned his memory. "There were two men from Villmark talking to him. Arguing, really."

"In Villmark?" I asked.

But he didn't seem to hear me. His eyes were still fixed on his own lap. "Two men. One with brown hair and brown eyes and a loud sort of laugh. The other with dark blue eyes and blond hair cut close to his scalp."

"How old?" Loke asked.

Leifr barked out a laugh. "I have no idea. I just can't see things properly anymore, not things like that." But he gave it a moment's thought, looking at Loke, then me, then Signi carefully. "Older than you two. Not so old as Signi. But closer to you two, I think."

"Thirties?" Loke guessed.

But Leifr just shrugged, giving up.

"How were they dressed?" Loke asked.

"Not like you," he said at once. Which didn't help. No one dressed like Loke. Then he turned to me and looked over my sweater and jeans. "Not like you or Signi. Or me, in what Signi's given me."

"Villmarker, then?" Loke asked.

But Leifr just scrunched up his face in frustration. "Not like they dressed in Villmark when I was young. I don't know."

"It's all right," Signi assured him, patting his knee again.

"It sounds like Raggi and Báfurr to me," Loke said.

"It sounds too vague to be sure to me," I countered.

"It's the best I can do," Leifr said, and his hands curled into fists again.

"We can work with it," Loke assured him. "So when was this?"

"A few days ago."

"Two?"

"I guess," Leifr said. "I didn't imagine it."

"I never thought you did," Loke said.

"Where was it?" I pressed.

"Somewhere I was," Leifr said, but his voice was starting to waver.

"You only wander through the woods and meadows, right? Not into town?"

"I go where I go," Leifr said. "I go here and there. Mostly here. Sometimes there."

"Leifr, it's all right," Signi said again. "Take all the time you need to center yourself."

"I'm fine!" he snapped at her. But she was unbothered by his response.

"Can I have a moment alone with Leifr?" Loke asked.

"Sure," I said at once, but Signi looked nervous at the thought of leaving Leifr's side.

"Just a moment," Loke said in his most charming voice.

"That doesn't work on me, Mr. Grímsson," she said sternly. But she did get up, waving for me to follow her to the kitchen.

"What was that?" I asked. I was thinking of what she had just said to Loke, but she misunderstood me.

"Leifr is doing much better since he got here, but this does happen," she said. She started tidying up her kitchen, and I stepped back and let her. I knew a calming ritual when I saw one. "Some stories he wants to tell, but if they have strong emotional components to them, they sort of slip away from him. His memory gets unmoored in time."

"So you knew he traveled through time?" I asked.

"I don't know if I'd call it that," she said as she moved the tea canister from the counter to its spot on the shelf over her stove. "I mean, we are all moving through time. He just kept doing it longer."

"But faster," I said. Then reconsidered. "Or slower?"

"It's all a bit beyond me," Signi said. "I just know when we try to talk about things that are triggers for him, he loses the details. Mostly it's time that he can't recall accurately, but sometimes it is locations." She gave me a sad look. "I'm sorry, I'm not sure how much help he'll be in your investigation. He could've seen the murder itself and not be able to tell you where or when it happened."

"I pretty much know where and when," I said. "It's who and why I'm working on."

"Ingrid, we're ready to go," Loke said suddenly from the doorway. Then he gave Signi his most charming smile again. "Thank you for your hospitality. I hope it won't be untoward if I drop in again? Just to visit with Leifr."

"That's up to Leifr," Signi said. But she sounded resigned, perhaps because we all knew what that answer would be.

"Did he tell you anything?" I whispered to Loke as I pulled on my jacket and hiking boots.

"About what?" Loke asked, maddeningly. "Oh, calm down. We have to go help Roarr get Odd into Villmark now, anyway. It's going to be dark soon."

I accepted that for the moment, but only because Signi and Leifr were both so close at hand, waiting to see us out the door.

But the moment we were outside, I asked, "so what did Signi mean when she said what you were doing wouldn't work on her? What was she talking about?"

"You know the answer to that, Ingy," he said. When I just glared at him, he laughed. "Come on! You know. My masculine wiles."

"You have wiles?" I asked.

"Some think so," he said, feigning hurt.

"And Leifr? Did he say anything at all?"

Loke went serious in the blink of an eye. "He definitely saw something. But it was a jumble. Come on, I was serious about hurrying to go help Roarr. But afterwards, I really think we should find Raggi and Báfurr."

"Fine," I said, but I wasn't looking forward to it.

Those two were pretty tired of being treated like suspects, and I could see their point.

If only they could stop being so suspicious-looking every time someone died.

CHAPTER TWELVE

WHEN I HAD FIRST COME to Villmark, Thorbjorn had warned me never to walk through the woods north of the village on my own. They were a dark, dangerous place that none but the Thors dared to venture into. He didn't have to warn me twice. At the time, I had felt a menacing presence every time I walked through those trees. Like I was being watched, tracked, hunted.

As Loke and I walked through them now in the growing darkness of sunset, it was hard to remember how wary I had been just a few months before. Granted, I wasn't alone now, and the one companion besides himself that Thorbjorn had allowed me was, in fact, Loke.

But a lot had changed since then. I had first learned that my latent magical abilities had made me a beacon, luring those dark forces I had felt hunting me. Then I had learned how to contain that glow. Even the most sensitive of creatures had to physically encounter me before they felt my magical presence. I was no longer walking around like the most delicious of bait.

But besides strengthening my magical defenses, I had learned a few ways to fight back when I needed to. Especially since the dwarves under the mountain had gifted me with a bronze wand.

Now, walking through those woods was no more dangerous than walking through the streets of Villmark.

Actually, it was probably safer. Bears were rare and kept to themselves, unlike the Villmarkers, who made no effort to conceal their feelings that I didn't belong among them.

But that feeling of safety was dashed when we reached the edge of the forest and found the cart tucked behind a cluster of trees and Roarr nowhere in sight.

"The body is still here," Loke said, lifting the tarp to be sure.

Mjolner meowed loudly to let us know he was still there as well.

"I'm sure with my grandmother's spells, he didn't even need to put it behind a tree to hide it from anyone's eyes but ours, but even so. He promised to stay with it," I said. "Where did he go?"

Loke peered through the trees, but I looked the other way, up the hill to the very edge of Villmark. I could see the tree that stood at the end of the northern-most road, and the roofline of the house where the Thors lived with their parents.

Then I saw the shadow of a figure come over the hill and head down towards us.

"Is that Roarr?" I asked Loke, even as my hand reached into my art bag to find my wand.

"Sure enough," Loke said. "He's got some explaining to do, for sure."

"Hey," Roarr said when he was close enough to see us standing in the shadows of the trees.

"Hey? Where were you?" I asked.

"I was having dinner with Valki and Gunna," he said.

"You said you'd wait with the body," I reminded him.

"Mjolner said it was fine," Roarr said defensively.

"Mjolner said—" I started to repeat, but then broke off in confusion. "He's a cat. How did he tell you anything?"

"That way he does," Roarr said vaguely.

"Never mind that. Why did you go into town?" Loke asked. "Please tell me it wasn't just because you were hungry."

"Not after that breakfast Nora gave us," Roarr said. "I was still thinking about who might have been in the woods when we were coming back from the cabin on Wednesday."

"The wyldemen," I said.

"Were they?" he asked.

"Yes, but they weren't much help," I admitted.

"Well, I felt useless just waiting here with the cart, so I went to talk to Valki about the patrols. He's in charge of that schedule, you know. Dinner just sort of happened."

"What did you tell him?" I asked.

"Everything," Roarr admitted. "He's on the council. He had to know."

"Fair enough," I said.

"He went to tell Brigida to prepare her room to receive his body first, then he's coming back here so the two of us can wheel the cart to her house," Roarr said.

"So what did he say when you told him about Odd?" Loke asked.

"He already knew he was in the area," Roarr said. "Or at least he'd heard rumors to that effect. Everyone volunteering for patrols seemed to be whispering about it. He had been ranging out more himself, hoping to find Odd before he actually appeared in town, but he never came far enough north to cross paths with him."

"Was he going to try to drive him off or what?" Loke asked.

"I don't know if he even knew. Just talk to him, I guess," Roarr said. "I was still a kid when Odd came to town last, so I guess I didn't realize, but every time Odd comes into town, he gets the disgruntled elements more riled up. It takes the council some time to settle everyone back down after he goes."

"This is an isolationist thing, isn't it?" I said with a sigh. "Odd is so separate from the outside world that Villmark is too close to it for his tastes."

"And rumors of his approach are enough to get people talking about making a change. Removing the council. That sort of thing," Loke said. "I'm no fan of the council myself, but if the alternative is the likes of Odd and his acolytes… Well, no thanks."

"Any idea when those rumors started?" I asked.

"Definitely after Wednesday," Roarr said. "And Valki was sure that Raggi and Báfurr were the two who started the whispering. Then we checked the schedule book, and they were on patrol together in the section of forest we would've been passing through on Wednesday."

"I told you they were involved in this," Loke said.

"Everything is pointing that way," I said. "I guess we find them and talk to them. Any idea where they are now?"

"Báfurr is out on patrol again, but Raggi has the night off," Roarr said.

"So he could be anywhere," I said.

"Not really," Loke said. "We know his haunts."

"More than that," Roarr said. "He's been seen hanging around Frigg quite a bit. I'll wait here for Valki, but you two should start at the bakery. If you find Frigg, you'll find Raggi."

Loke and I headed up the hill and then down into town. I had never been to the bakery run by the sisters known collectively as the Freyas, although I had eaten their bread often enough to know just how excellent it was.

The sisters were cousins to the Thors, and like the Thors, there had been five of them until the ill-fated hunting expedition we had all taken together months before. Now, thanks to the Wild Hunt and a man with access to magic he shouldn't have had, there were only three.

Everything after the Wild Hunt had been such a jumble of activity, though. Thorbjorn and I had never gone back to the lodge after we had lured the Hunt away from it. Then the Thors had gone north, and I had gone to Runde for just one night that had ended in the whirlwind of yet another murder investigation.

Ever since proving my grandmother innocent of the murder that happened in her mead hall, I had been up north at Frór's isolated cabin. While I had mostly fixated on how that kept me apart from my Runde friends and from my Villmarker friends, the truth was I also hadn't actually seen any of the Freyas since we had caught the man who had been luring them out to be captured by the Wild Hunt.

So I had no idea if they blamed me for their sisters' deaths.

"Are you okay?" Loke asked me as he lead the way down the long downhill road to the south end of town.

"Yeah. Just thinking about everything that went on last December," I said. Then I gave him an accusing look. "You missed it."

"I've heard all about it," he said. "From you, from Nora, and from half of Villmark. You haven't been here, but it's quite a tale in all the halls. Raggi and Báfurr have been drinking for free on the strength of that story all winter."

"In what way?" I asked, not sure I wanted to know.

"Actually, even in their tellings, you come off well," he said. "It helps that you were gone that last night. Left them some space for valor."

"I don't actually know what happened when I was gone," I admitted. "Thorbjorn came to find me. Outside of that, I never got the story."

"Maybe get it from Kara and Nilda," he suggested.

"Sure, when they're not busy," I said, more glumly than I had intended.

"They guard the ancestral fire," Loke said. "I'm sure they'd appreciate a little company while doing it. It's not like that duty consumes all their faculties."

"I suppose. I don't know if all this is going to end with me back in town or not, though. My grandmother hasn't said a thing about being ready to come home yet," I said.

"Give her time," Loke said, then gestured to a building on across the street from the public garden. "There it is."

My heart sank. The windows were dark. We were too late. They had closed.

But then someone came out the door, turning at once to lock it behind them. I could tell it was a woman, but under the voluminous hood and cloak, I couldn't guess who.

"Frigg?" I said hopefully as Loke and I drew closer.

But when she turned around, I saw it was Freydis, one of the older sisters. Her cheeks were rounder than I remembered, but not so much rounder as her belly. She had barely been showing the last time I'd seen her, but she was clearly in her last trimester now.

She just stared at me for a minute, but then tears sprang from her eyes and she lunged at me. I recoiled defensively, but she wasn't attacking me.

She was hugging me.

Really tight. But still, just a hug.

"Ingrid," she said. "It's been so long. We were starting to worry you'd never return."

"No, I'm just tending to my grandmother for a while," I said, patting her shoulder somewhat awkwardly. She finally let me go, wiping at her eyes.

"Sorry. Hormones," she said, and gave me a teary smile. "Are you here for bread? We don't have much left, but whatever we have is yours, of course."

"No, we're not here for bread," I said.

"Right," she said. "You said Frigg's name. Are you looking for her?"

"To start with," I said.

"She left just a couple of minutes ago. With Raggi," Freydis said. "They were going to take a walk, but it's starting to get chilly out here. I wouldn't be surprised if they ducked into Aldís' mead hall instead."

"That's a walk from here just to get there," Loke said, taking half a step back to look up the street we'd just come down. We would've noticed if the two of them had passed us on the main road. They must've taken a more roundabout way.

"Is this for another investigation?" Freydis asked, half eagerness to help, half worry that her sister was involved.

"We wanted to talk to Raggi," I said, not exactly answering her question.

But she just nodded. "If I see her before you do, I'll let her know. But I'm heading home now to get off my feet, so I probably won't run into her. But best of luck. And do stop by in the morning sometime. Any of us Freyas would love to shower you with fresh bread, anytime!"

"I'll remember that," I promised her.

She watched Loke and I walk past the main road, continuing on into the western half of town. I looked back before we turned north, and she gave me one last wave before turning to head home.

"She sort of acted like you weren't there," I said to Loke.

"Fine with me," he said with a shrug.

For my part, I was just relieved that the sisters weren't angry with me over what had happened. Not that I would blame them if they were. If I had figured things out sooner, I could've saved more than just Kara.

"There they are," Loke said, pointing up ahead of us. I saw two figures standing in the middle of the road. They were both cloaked, standing so close that the folds of their cloaks were intermingling. I could tell it was a man and a woman, but I couldn't discern any features within the shadows of their hoods.

But they stepped apart as we drew closer, and I saw first Raggi's scowling face and then Frigg's startled one. But she quickly shifted from startled to embarrassed, looking away from me and taking half a step back. But back from me or from Raggi, I couldn't quite tell.

"What do you want?" Raggi asked in a long-suffering tone.

"You'd never believe it, but we have some questions for you," Loke said.

Raggi's scowl deepened. "About what?"

"Something we'd rather keep private, at least for the moment," I said as diplomatically as I could.

"Is that so?" he asked, folding his arms as if preparing to become an unmoveable obstacle.

But Frigg was taking yet another step away from him. "I should go," she said.

"What? Why?" he demanded.

"She said it was private," Frigg said to him. Then she gave me a pleading look. "I should go. But it's good to see you, Ingrid. Truly."

"When I'm back at home, I'll be sure to stop by the bakery and say a proper hello to you all," I promised.

She gave me a wide, if tremulous, smile. "That would be lovely."

Then she turned and left, all but fleeing back down the road.

"This had better be good," Raggi growled at us. His arms were still crossed, his feet planted well apart.

I wasn't trying to physically get past him, but I was sure he was just as prepared to block me in whatever I wanted to do.

I took a deep breath and prepared to once again to wage a battle of words with him.

But Loke spoke before I could even start. "Let me buy you an ale."

"One ale?" Raggi asked, lifting a single eyebrow.

"I'll keep buying you ales so long as you keep answering Ingrid's questions," he said.

Raggi glared at him for a long moment, then said, "deal."

He turned and led the way uphill to Aldís' mead hall.

CHAPTER THIRTEEN

I HAD BEEN INSIDE ALDÍS' mead hall only once before. Most nights, when I wasn't home, I was at my grandmother's mead hall that stood on the border of Villmark and Runde, where the two populations mixed without the people of Runde even realizing it. But that building stood cold and dark now, waiting for her and her magic to return.

Since moving to Villmark, I had frequented Ullr's mead hall near the southern public gardens, quite close to the Freyas' bakery. There was no actual magic there, but it was large and brightly lit and mostly filled by people who were friendly to me.

Aldís' mead hall, on the other hand, was low-roofed and dark even during the day. And the people who drank there were decidedly unfriendly to me. The Villmarkers who frowned on any interaction between their community and Runde favored that hall, and I was the living symbol of that interaction even more than my own grandmother was.

So the minute we stepped inside, I could feel all eyes on me. I couldn't see them, not in that gloom, not with nearly every patron shrouded in shadows with their hoods up over their heads like they were all there to plot crimes.

But I was there with Raggi. That afforded me some measure of protection. That was probably the only reason why I wasn't confronted the minute I came in the door.

Raggi led Loke and me to an empty table, the very table we had questioned him at when I had been in here before. The rest of the mead hall was filled with people, some crowding so close there was no room for elbows around their tables. So this one had been left empty on purpose. Just for him.

"Aldís, a pitcher of ale," he called as he sat with his back to the wall. Loke and I sat across from him. Loke sat sideways on his chair, keeping his eyes both on Raggi and on the room behind us. But I leaned in over the table to face Raggi more directly. I wanted him to know I was focused just on him.

Even if that wasn't quite true. My magical senses were on full alert. There was no one under that roof with a touch of magic to them, but I could sense even mundane activity when I was that keyed up. No one was going to sneak up on me.

"We need to talk about what happened on Wednesday," I said, but Raggi immediately lifted a finger to silence me.

"You said you'd answer our questions," Loke said.

"Do you see any ale before me yet?" Raggi asked.

So we sat in silence until Aldís arrived with a pitcher full of foaming ale and a single mug. She set them both in front of Raggi and left without asking Loke or me if we wanted anything.

I watched as Raggi poured ale into the mug, then took a long drink. Then another. After a third, he set the mug down and wiped the foam from his beard and mustache.

"Ready?" Loke asked him.

"Nothing happened on Wednesday," Raggi said, then reached for the pitcher to top off his mug.

"I know you know Odd Oddsen was in the area," I told him. "I want to know how you knew that. Did you meet with him?"

"Maybe the crows told me," Raggi said.

"Maybe you overheard Roarr and I in the forest while you were out on patrol," Loke suggested.

"Like I've got nothing better to do while out on patrol than eavesdrop on you and your friend," Raggi said with a smirk.

"Do you?" Loke asked with feigned surprise. "From what I've heard, no one on any patrol has come across anything since the Thors left."

"Our mere presence is keeping trouble at bay," Raggi said.

"Is that so?" Loke asked. "Interesting."

"I won't sit here and have my service maligned by a bystander," Raggi growled at me.

"I think we're getting off topic here," I said to Loke. Then to Raggi, "so you're admitting that you knew Odd was in the area?"

"Rumor has it he was coming into Villmark soon," Raggi said, and took another sip of the ale.

"Rumors you spread," Loke said.

"Is that what you're accusing me of? Spreading rumors?" Raggi asked. "And if Odd were in the area and was planning on coming into Villmark too, anyone who told others about that could hardly be considered to be spreading rumors, could they?"

"He was staying at Frór's cabin with my grandmother and I. Did you know that?" I asked him.

Raggi shrugged and signalled for Aldís to bring him another pitcher of ale.

"I'm not sure he was intending to come into town at all. He was certainly in no hurry to leave our company. I think it was likely he only wanted to speak with my grandmother, not with anyone else," I said.

"What does that have to do with me?" Raggi asked as he poured the last of the first pitcher into his mug.

"Odd hasn't been here in more than a decade. Were you looking forward to seeing him?" I asked.

"It's a bit of an event," he said noncommittally.

"Did you go out to find him, perchance?" I asked.

"Why would I do that?" he asked.

"You and Báfurr?" I pressed.

"I don't know what you two are on about," he said. "Báfurr and I patrolled together on Wednesday. We were in the woods north of the village. We saw nothing, and we reported nothing. You can check the patrol logs."

"We already have," Loke said, which I guessed was technically true. Valki had likely shown them to Roarr when they were looking at the schedules. If they had contained anything worth knowing, Roarr would've passed it on.

"And now here I am, having my one night off thoroughly ruined by you two, and Báfurr is off patrolling again with Manni in pretty much the same section of forest. So what exactly am I being accused of?" Raggi asked.

"Do you feel accused?" I asked.

"By you? Always," he said and took another drink of ale.

I sighed and slumped back in my chair. I briefly entertained the hope he'd be easier to talk to with another couple of pitchers of ale in him, but his mood was already souring. More ale might just make him more combative.

Then someone else came into the hall, bringing a gust of chill air in with them that set all the candles fluttering. Raggi looked up past Loke and I. The look on his face was a puzzled frown before he turned his attention back to his ale.

But Loke, still sitting sideways, poked me in the ribs. I turned to see Leifr, unfortunately still decked out in all the best windproof clothing the world of Runde could provide, crossing the room to us. If he even noticed all the glares directed his way, he paid them no attention at all.

"Ingrid. I've been looking for you everywhere," he said. His voice sounded relieved, but his expression and body language were still all agitated. "I have things straight in my head now. I can tell you everything."

"Can it wait a moment?" I asked him.

He looked crushed, but he nodded.

Then he looked up and noticed Raggi for the first time. His eyes narrowed at once, his skin darkening to an angry purple.

"You!" he hissed.

"What?" Raggi asked. I could see his annoyance at being accosted by a man dressed in clothes from Runde in his safe Villmarkers-only space. But past that, his confusion was real.

He genuinely didn't seem to know Leifr at all.

"You were there!" Leifr said, stabbing a finger at Raggi. "You saw everything."

"I don't know what you're talking about," Raggi said. But it wasn't so much a denial as a command. A threat.

But Leifr didn't hear that tone. "You were there with that other man, arguing in the rain with Odd Oddsen."

I realized in that moment that the soft murmur of voices around us had only been people pretending to have their own conversations. Because the minute that name rang out, they all fell silent, no longer caring if we knew they were all listening in.

There was also a lot of shifting around. No one was armed with axes or swords, not in this tight space, but no Villmarker went anywhere without at least one knife and more often two. That shifting around felt too much to me like a lot of people throwing back their cloaks off their shoulders, making sure those knives were in easy reach.

But I didn't dare turn to look. I didn't want to take my eyes off Raggi's face.

"You're that crazy fellow," Raggi said slowly, as if he was just putting it together. "I've heard about you. Stark raving mad, you are."

"I'm lucid enough," Leifr said. "I know what I saw. And so do you. You were there."

I really wanted to pull Leifr aside, to get his whole story without an audience. But I was afraid if I did that, Raggi would just disappear. He had done it before.

"What did you see, Leifr?" Loke asked, not even bothering to lower his voice.

Whatever Leifr said now, it would be all over Villmark by morning. That Odd Oddsen had been there, that he was dead now.

That he had been murdered.

"I saw this man and his friend out on the promontory by Ingrid's cabin, arguing in the rain," he said.

Raggi scoffed. "He doesn't even know my name."

"I know your face," Leifr said.

"When was this?" Loke asked.

"When Odd fell," Leifr said. "I got it jumbled up in my head before, but it's all straight now. If I think about things calmly, I can get them straight in my head."

I wanted to put my face in my hands in despair at what the whisper network was going to do with this bit of information.

But Loke just nodded gravely. "I know how it is," he said. "Go on."

"I saw them arguing. This man and his friend wanted Odd to do something he didn't want to do." Leifr coughed out a laugh. "Like anyone can get Odd to do anything he doesn't want to do. Ever."

"What did they want him to do?" Loke asked.

"I didn't hear that part. Only that Odd said no," Leifr said. "Then he turned to walk away, back to the cabin. Only this guy's friend tried to catch his arm and pull him back. Make him listen to what he had to say."

Raggi scoffed again, but I shot him a quelling glare. I must've put a little magical bite to it without realizing it, because he lapsed back into silence, turning his attention back to his ale.

"What happened then?" Loke asked.

"He tried to grab Odd's arm, his forearm, to turn him around. But Odd did this snakey move, slipped right out of his grip. But the moment his arm was free, Odd struck the man with his palm right in the middle of his chest. It was a quick little strike. Again, like a snake. But it staggered that guy back several paces. And everything was slick because the rain was turning to ice, and he nearly fell back over the edge."

Raggi pressed a hand over his eyes, but said nothing.

"He caught his balance?" I asked.

"No, Odd caught him by the front of his shirt and pulled him back. He made sure the guy was standing on his own two feet. Then he let him go. But before he could walk away again, the man pushed him. Hard. With both hands. Right over the side."

"Was it an accident?" I asked, just because I had to be sure. "The edge of the cliff crumbled away. Did Báfurr push him onto the ledge and then it fell?"

"No," Leifr said, glaring at Raggi even as Raggi continued to cover his face, as if tuning us all out. "No, he shoved Odd hard enough to push him over the edge. Odd almost caught himself right there on the precipice. He sort of hovered for a moment at this impossible angle. Like he was using the air and the rain and the wind off the lake to get himself back up on his feet somehow."

Leifr swallowed hard, then looked around us as if noticing the rapt audience to his words for the first time. "I'm not crazy," he said.

"I know," Loke said.

"It was murder," Leifr said firmly. "This man and his friend murdered Odd Oddsen, and I saw it with my own two eyes."

Raggi sat motionless in his chair, but both of his hands were pressed to his eyes now.

Leifr turned to me, all of his anger spent, and said, "you know where to find me if you need me, but I should get back now. She doesn't know I came here."

"Yes, go home, Leifr," I said. I could only imagine what would run through Signi's mind if she even suspected that Leifr had come into town.

He nodded again, and Loke gave him a reassuring pat on the shoulder. Then he was gone. But the tension in the room remained.

"Raggi?" I said.

He lowered his hands. His eyes were red-rimmed, but what I saw within them was grief and anger in almost equal portions.

"Fine," he spat at me. "Báfurr did it. Happy?"

As if such news could make anyone happy.

CHAPTER FOURTEEN

I SAT BACK in my chair and regarded Raggi. After metaphorically dropping the mic after that last remark, he was now studiously pretending I wasn't even there, ignoring me even as I studied him. I remembered every time I had crossed paths with him before.

He hadn't killed Gullveig.

He hadn't even been involved with what happened to Nefja.

And we had been something close to comrades-in-arms against the Wild Hunt at the hunting lodge last December.

Still, something just wouldn't let me trust the guy, let alone like him. As abrasive and combative as he was every single time I dealt with him, I was pretty sure that wasn't what left me so unsettled after being in his company.

On impulse, I took out my sketchbook and drew him sitting there, nursing an ale and not looking at me. Loke watched over my shoulder but said nothing.

When I was done, I looked the sketch over. It was all dark, angry lines that bit deep into the paper, almost tearing it in places. Raggi was an angry man, angry on a deeper level than I had recognized before. It had made sense before, his anger the first time I had met him. He had loved Gullveig, had proposed to her twice and been spurned twice.

Then she had been murdered by the outsider she had chosen over him. Of course, he had been angry about that.

But looking at the sketch now and the man before me as well, I realized that anger went deeper than I had initially thought.

What was its root?

I took out my wand and waved it in the air between us, letting my eyes go unfocused.

"Hey!" he objected, deigning to notice me again. He reached across the table but didn't dare to touch that wand. He just seized my wrist, squeezing it harder than he needed to just to stop the motion.

"Let her go," Loke said, his voice deep and dangerous in a way I had never heard from him before. He even moved as if to reach for a knife I knew he wasn't wearing.

But Raggi let me go. I was pretty sure his grip was going to leave a mark, but I resisted the urge to rub the skin.

"I was just looking at you," I said. "You've seen me use this wand before. I don't hurt people with it. You know that."

"Maybe I just don't want you looking at me like that," he said. "Put it away."

I felt again all the menace of the room around us. I put the wand away.

"Hiding something, are you?" Loke asked.

"What more is there to hide? I just told you everything," he said.

"You told us what Báfurr did. Not what you did," I pointed out.

"I did nothing at all," he said.

"You were there for a reason," I said.

"It's not like you can lie to her, you know," Loke said.

Raggi looked stricken, as if that thought hadn't occurred to him before. I was pretty sure it was possible to lie to me. People did it all the time. But Raggi took Loke completely seriously.

"Báfurr and I heard Loke and Roarr talking about Odd Oddsen in the woods," he said, gripping the sides of his ale mug so tightly his knuckles turned white. "We knew where he was. And I was pretty sure I knew the way to Frór's cabin."

"What did you hear specifically?" I asked.

"Really, just that he was there," he insisted. "But that's all we needed to know."

"It's what you were waiting for," Loke guessed.

"Waiting?" Raggi repeated.

"For him to lead you or whatever," Loke said dismissively.

"We don't need anyone to lead us," Raggi said. "We do as we please."

"But you wanted him to act against the council, didn't you?" I said.

Raggi chewed at his lip. "Look, none of us really cares about the council. They don't govern our lives. We do as we please."

"So you've said," Loke said.

"But others do listen to the council," I said. "You wanted to change that."

"We weren't planning to do anything against the laws of Villmark," Raggi said. "But we're allowed to think that things can be handled differently. Better. We're allowed to say that to each other. We're allowed to work to affect change."

"You wanted Odd Oddsen to come here and throw the council out?" I asked again.

"We just wanted him to come into town and meet with all of us. To talk with us," he said.

"And if that talk led to violence?" Loke asked.

Raggi glared at him. "You make so many assumptions."

"Let's stick with what actually happened," I said, putting a hand up to belay any more fighting between them. "You wanted Odd to come into town and speak with you and your friends. And you knew how to find him. So you and Báfurr came out to the cabin to talk with him."

"More or less," Raggi said.

Loke opened his mouth to speak, but I shook my head at him and he fell silent again.

"I'm guessing that what Leifr told us is true, then," I said. "You spoke with Odd about coming into town, and he turned you down. But Báfurr didn't want to take no for an answer."

"It wasn't like that," Raggi said. "He just wanted a chance to make our case fully. Odd was saying no before he even heard what we had to say."

"I wonder why?" Loke asked idly.

"And the rest of it? The shoving back and forth? That's how it all happened?" I asked.

"I don't know about that last bit. I didn't see the air hold him up or whatever that kid was going on about. But the rest of it, yes," Raggi said.

"Odd saved Báfurr's life, then," I said. "And Báfurr returned the favor by pushing him to his death."

"No," Raggi said, but slowly, like he was honestly thinking it through. "I don't think Báfurr thought that's what was going to happen. First of all, it all happened a lot faster than Leifr was telling it."

Then he reached across the table to snatch Loke's arm. Loke pulled away, but Raggi pulled him closer, halfway across the table, before shoving him back again. Loke fell back onto his chair, nearly toppling out of it as it was still positioned sideways to the table.

"Like that," Raggi said, taking another sip of ale. "Boom, boom, boom. Move and countermove. Too fast for thinking."

"Báfurr was the aggressor. Twice," I said.

"Yeah, but not like you're making it sound," Raggi said.

"Like what then?" I asked as reasonably as I could.

"Look, Odd is this figure that looms larger than life, right? He fights giants. He slays dragons. You know? And compared to him, we're all weak little children."

"He wasn't exactly young," I said.

"No, he was ageless," Raggi said. "Ageless, not old. Did he look like an old man to you? I'm not talking about the silver in his hair or the wrinkles in his skin."

"No, I know what you mean," I admitted. "He looked like he could plant his feet and nothing could move him."

"Exactly," Raggi said.

"But when Báfurr grabbed him, he was walking away. His feet weren't planted. And when he shoved him?"

Raggi sighed. "I really don't think Báfurr expected him to move an inch. He assumed when he pushed, that Odd would just stand there like a boulder, unmoved. Why do you think he used both hands?"

"If he didn't expect any of it to do any good, why do it at all, though?" I asked. "Why shove a mountain?"

"Obviously, Báfurr is a hothead," Raggi said.

Loke started to laugh but turned it into a very unconvincing cough. I smiled inwardly myself. It was a real pot calling the kettle black situation, Raggi calling Báfurr a hothead.

Especially when he glared daggers at us like that.

"Sorry," I said, forcing myself back into neutral investigative mode.

"Look, we went out there to talk with him," Raggi said. "Neither of us wanted him dead. Even you would have to admit that doesn't make any sense. It doesn't move us closer to any of our goals. It's just wasteful. It was an accident. A tragic accident."

"You're sure?" Loke asked. "You talked to Báfurr about it after and he told you?"

"I saw it on his face," Raggi said darkly. "I saw the look in his eyes when Odd fell back, and the look when he lunged forward to try to catch him and failed. And yes, Báfurr tried to save him. But the rock crumbled away, and I had to pull him back or they both would've gone over."

"But you didn't talk to him after?" I asked.

"We were both more than a little numb," Raggi said. "Not all of us deal with death up close and personal over and over again like you do."

"Well, there's no arguing with that," Loke said to me. But this time, his stab at humor just left me cold.

"I'd like to talk to Báfurr himself about all this," I said.

"I'd like that too," Raggi said. "He certainly won't talk to me about it. And you, as a volva, could absolve him, couldn't you?"

"If I felt like he merited it," I said. Assuming Raggi meant in the eyes of the council, I could speak on his behalf. If he meant absolve him in the eyes of the gods, I didn't know who could do that.

"Well, I don't know where he is now, beyond patrolling with Manni," Raggi said. "I wish I could help you."

Now all his sincerity was gone, and I could feel that brief moment of openness fading away. The old animosity was back.

"That's all right," I said as I got up from the table. "I think Loke and I can take it from here. Thanks for your help."

Raggi made a noncommittal grunt, but just as I was turning to leave, he added, "I was angry with him, too. Odd Oddsen, I mean. He's let us all down. But that won't matter soon."

I knew he was addressing the room around us more than me specifically. And I suppose I was doing the same when I turned back to ask him, "because he'll be back soon?"

"What? No. He's dead. Surely he's dead," he said, his voice lifting ever so slightly at the end of that sentence.

"He's dead," I confirmed.

"We'll carry on without him, then," Raggi said.

Loke and I left him there with the remains of his pitcher of ale. Loke tossed a few coins to Aldís on our way out.

I wasn't sure what to make of that last exchange. In a way, it was heartening that Raggi and the others weren't expecting Odd to rise from the dead and lead them again.

On the other hand, whoever they chose to lead them next was almost certainly not going to be an improvement. A leader who refused to give in to their demands, who spent more time away than among them, was infinitely preferable to what would surely come next.

But like Raggi said, such things were not against any laws. Things were going to get harder in Villmark.

And there was nothing I could do to stop it, even if I wanted to.

CHAPTER FIFTEEN

ᚠ

WE STEPPED out of the close interior of Aldís's mead hall, back into the chilly March night. The last of the clouds had dispersed, and the moon and stars shone brightly, lighting up the icy roads around us. We could follow the main road to the center of town, take it the other direction out to the wilderness west of the town, or duck down any of the many alleys that ran uphill to the north or downhill to the south.

But I stood frozen in place, unsure of which way to go or what to do next.

"Raggi really upset you," Loke said beside me. He had his bare hands plunged deep into the pockets of his pants and was hunched over a bit, as if that could compensate for his lack of coat.

"If Báfurr didn't mean to do it, that makes this manslaughter and not murder, right?" I said.

Loke shrugged. "Those are Runde concepts. Here, it will be up to the council to decide his fate. And it matters more what he did after Odd fell than what he did before."

"What do you mean?" I asked.

"Like I've told you before, two men get into a fight in the heat of passion and one of them ends up dead is not against the law here," he said. "You have to make restitution to the family now short a member, but beyond that, life just goes on."

"Odd had no family," I said.

"Right. So in this case, it would just be a matter of Báfurr presenting himself to the council and confessing what he did. The important thing is that everything is out in the open. Everyone in Villmark has to know what happened and how and why."

"But this happened days ago, and Báfurr hasn't said anything," I said.

"Yeah, that's bad for Báfurr," Loke said. "But the council still might have leniency for him. If he's upset and out of sorts and just doesn't have his head right yet, they'll understand. But the time for that is running out."

"He's out on patrol now," I said. "So, do we track him down, or do we wait?"

"I guess that's up to you as the volva," Loke said. "If you track him down and drag him back, that's going to play out differently for him than if he came back and turned himself in."

"But if he was going to do that, wouldn't he have done it already?" I asked.

"Maybe he was hoping this would all just go away," Loke said with another shrug. "Listen, why don't you go back to your house and wait?" I made a face, but he put up a hand to keep me from interrupting him. "I'll go find Roarr, and we'll be waiting for Báfurr when he comes back from this patrol. We'll talk him into turning himself in if he's still on the fence about it. Give him one last chance to do the right thing."

"Which can't be done the same way if I'm there because I'm the volva," I sighed. "I guess I understand. But I really don't feel like walking all the way back to the cabin and leaving this so undone still."

"I wasn't talking about going back to Frór's place," Loke said with a grin. "Did you forget you have a place in town?"

I hadn't forgotten, but I hadn't been thinking of it, either.

"Right," I said. "I'll go there. I want to do some more meditating and drawing, actually. My mind is terribly unsettled, and I need to get some things straight with myself. But come and find me once you and Roarr talk to Báfurr."

"Of course," Loke said, then looked around, head tipped back as if he were smelling for something in the air. Then he strolled off to the north end of town.

I turned to the east and followed the main east-west road to the square at the center of the village, then turned south and walked past a few houses before reaching my own. The house my grandmother had grown up in, now mine.

I wasn't surprised to see Mjolner there waiting for me on the front step. He always seemed to know where I was going before I did. But I was surprised to see that he wasn't waiting alone.

Someone sat beside him on the frigid front step, a woman in a long cloak with the fur-lined hood drawn close around her face. She was hunched over, face in her hands as if overcome with emotion.

But I recognized the braids of dark blonde hair that draped forward over her shoulders.

"Kara?" I called, rushing through the gate and up the path through the front garden.

She heard me call her name and lifted her head to look at me. She hadn't been crying, but I could tell by the redness of her eyes that she had been fighting doing just that for quite some time.

"Ingrid," she said with a tremulous smile. "I heard you were in town, but I didn't know where you were. Then Mjolner brought me here, but you weren't home."

"No, but he knew I would be," I said, opening my front door and hustling us all into the mudroom. I pried off my boots, then glided into the living room in my stockinged feet to get a fire going, not bothering to take off my jacket or hat first.

Kara took off her boots and cloak, then followed me into the living room, Mjolner close on her heels. She was still dressed for her duty of guarding the ancestral fire, wearing the more traditional homespun Villmarker clothing with leather gauntlets protecting her forearms and a pair of long knives at her belt.

"It will warm up quickly," I promised as I added sticks to the kindling, then after another moment one of the logs from the rack on the hearth.

"I'm not cold," Kara said. "And I only have a minute to talk to you. I have to get back to Nilda at the fire before midnight."

"It's nearly midnight already?" I sighed. No wonder I felt so bone-tired. But I still had meditation and drawing to do before I could even think of napping.

"The nights are getting shorter," Kara said. It almost sounded ominous, the way she said it. I sat back from the fireplace to see her just sort of standing there like a zombie mid-shamble. I took her by the shoulders and guided her to a chair, then pulled another chair over to sit knee-to-knee to her.

"You're worried about Thorge," I said.

"I know it's too soon to expect them back," Kara said, too quickly. She'd been told that a lot lately, I was guessing.

"It's been more than two months," I said. "It's been weighing on my mind, too."

"Has it?" Kara asked eagerly.

"I expected to hear from them more," I admitted. "Although I don't know how they'd get word to us."

"So you're just worried? Like normal worried?" she asked, biting her lip.

"Aren't you?" I asked.

"It's more than that," she said darkly. Then she hugged herself, rubbing her arms as if feeling the chill even as the fire started driving it from the room.

"Loke mentioned you were feeling down. But it's more than that, isn't it?" I said.

"I've tried talking to Nilda about it. And she tries to help, she really does. But in the end, I can tell she just doesn't believe me," Kara said miserably.

"Believe you about what?" I asked.

She looked away from me, towards the flames dancing in the fire-place. Then she shuddered and squeezed her eyes shut, as if the sight of fire disturbed her.

"You've been seeing things in the ancestral fire," I guessed.

She opened her eyes to gape at me. Then she nodded slowly.

"But only volvas are supposed to be able to do that, and I'm no volva," Kara said.

"Let's not worry about why it's happening just now. Let's just accept that it is," I said. The look of relief on her face that I wasn't meeting her story with skepticism was so profound it made my heart ache. I put a hand on her knee and gave it a reassuring squeeze. "Tell me what you've seen."

"It started as just a feeling," she admitted. "An unease, like something was wrong, but it was so vague. That went on for weeks before I even started to feel like it had anything to do with Thorge and the others."

"Was there a specific thing that marked the change? Did anything happen that might have been a trigger?" I asked. She shook her head, but I persisted. "Did it change when my grandmother and I went north?"

"No, it was vague before and after that, and it only slowly grew more specific in my mind," Kara said. "I started having dreams. Nightmares, really. I didn't always remember them when I woke, but I know they were about Thorge being hunted by something. But I could never see what."

"How long have you been dreaming this?" I asked.

"I'm not sure. It didn't really start all at once," she admitted. "I was worried all the time, so it wasn't weird that I had upsetting dreams, you know?"

"I know," I said. "But something changed because you're talking to me now."

"I see things in the fire now," she said, her voice barely louder than a whisper. "For the last week, I've been seeing visions in the flames. Nilda keeps telling me it's just because I haven't been sleeping. Which is true, I haven't. But I can tell she isn't convinced herself that that's all it is."

"Visions of what?" I asked.

Kara made a frustrated, strangled sort of sound. "It's like the dreams. I know Thorge and the others are in danger. Something is hunting them, pursuing them, hiding from them. But I can't quite get a glimpse of it. I get so close to seeing it, and then the vision just melts away."

"So you've been staring into the flames more, trying to make the visions come back," I guessed. She nodded, but there was a questioning look on her face. I just shrugged. "It's what I would do."

"So you've not been having dreams at all about Thorbjorn or Thorge or anyone?" she asked.

"Not that I can recall," I said. I didn't want to admit that I hadn't had a dream that I could remember in quite some time. And that included after I had started working with the new rune. I had a sudden fear that something was blocking me. But was it something inside of me, or outside?

I shuddered at the thought.

"Ingrid?" Kara asked.

"I'm all right," I said.

"I really do have to get back," Kara said, getting up from the chair.

"I'm glad you took the time to track me down," I said as I walked with her to the door. "I'm waiting here for Loke and Roarr to find Báfurr, but in the meantime I have a little time on my hands. I'm going to meditate and draw and see what I get."

"Thank you," Kara said as she swung her cloak around her shoulders.

"In the meantime, try not to look into the flames," I said. "That fire has powerful magic. It's designed to protect the community, but it's still not to be trifled with."

She gave me a wan smile. "You're starting to sound like your grandmother," she said.

"I should hope so," I said. "Say hello to Nilda for me. I'll stop in and see you both before I go north again."

"You have to," Kara said firmly. "I need to know what you see. I need to know if I'm going crazy, or if I'm right and something is wrong out there."

"I'm going to look into it right now," I promised her. Neither of those possibilities were good.

I watched until Kara was past my front gate, then went back to the rug before the fireplace. Mjolner was there, but not in his cat bed. He was sitting primly, as if waiting for me to begin.

I had intended to meditate before the fire, then get up and move to the corner where my easel and supplies were, but something in the back of my mind was niggling. Like something big was about to burst and sweep over me.

So I grabbed my art bag instead and sat down on the rug with Mjolner pressed up against one knee and my sketchbook and pencils close to the other.

I took a deep breath, but never felt myself let it out again.

Because the minute I closed my eyes, I was just gone.

CHAPTER SIXTEEN

SOMETHING WAS MAKING my face all hot and tingling. That was the first thing I knew.

The second thing was that I was very, very thirsty. My tongue was thick and furry and my lips had been plastered together, then the plaster had dried and cracked. Nothing about that was remotely comfortable.

And someone was meowing my name.

No, Mjolner was meowing his most shrill, most demanding meow. But someone else was calling my name.

My eyes were even more crusted over than my mouth, but I managed to get them open even as I pushed away the hands that were shaking my shoulders.

"Stop," I grumbled, trying to sit up. That proved beyond me. So I slumped on my side on the floor instead. I had moved away from the hands, but now I was in the full light of the morning sun, so bright it hurt my eyes.

"If I didn't know better, I'd think she'd been drinking," Loke said laughingly.

"Stop it. This is serious," Roarr said. He was walking towards me.

He squatted between me and the window, mercifully blocking out the sun, and brought the rim of a glass of water to my lips.

I took it from him and chugged it down so fast it made my stomach cramp. But then I thrust the glass back at him and waved for him to bring me some more.

"What exactly happened in here?" Loke asked as I rubbed the crust from my eyes and made another go at sitting up.

"What do you mean? I guess I fell asleep at some point," I confessed. I hadn't intended to do that. Meditation and drawing, that had been the first two orders of business. But the nap had won out, apparently.

"I'm not surprised you needed a rest after all this," Loke said. Confused, I turned to put my back to the window and finally got a look at my living room.

It was covered in paper. Sheets of various sizes were draped over absolutely everything, and the floor was littered with sketchbooks left laying open and a scattering of broken pencils and charcoal sticks.

And every page was covered with drawing. I picked up the nearest page, and then another and another. Every page, front and back, was covered in dense sketches, one sketch layered on top of another.

"What happened?" I asked.

"That's what we were asking you," Loke said.

"I don't remember any of this," I said. I shivered, and he pushed a stack of loose papers off the couch to fetch a blanket for me. But the sun-drenched room was plenty warm.

It was my soul that was cold.

"What happened?" I asked again. Roarr returned with the second glass of water and I took it from him. This one I managed to drink in respectable sips.

"I'm guessing all of this wasn't just about finding Báfurr," Loke said as he started gathering up pages into stacks. Roarr quickly fell in to doing the same. I reached for the nearest sketchbook and turned the pages as I kept taking sips of water.

"I don't think so," I said.

"What were you focused on?" Loke asked. I set the chaos of a sketchbook aside and was about to try standing up again when Mjolner jumped onto my lap and curled up there, making a dead weight of himself. Clearly, he didn't think I was ready to get up yet.

"Finding Báfurr was maybe third on my list of priorities," I admitted. "Kara told me about some dreams and visions she's been having, so that was the second thing on my mind."

"And the first?" Loke asked.

"Odd," I said slowly. It was like saying the words was summoning the memories. I didn't know what I remembered until I heard myself say it out loud. "No, really, it was about the runes in general, and the rune ase in particular, but also an argument that Odd had made that I was going about learning the runes all wrong."

"How would he know?" Loke asked.

"I guess he knew them all," Roarr said to him. "Even if he wasn't as closely associated with Odin as he wanted us all to believe, even if it was all in his head, he would learn the runes just as part of that. Wouldn't he?"

"I think so," I said. "But I never saw him use any magic. He was definitely suffused with magic, but I never saw him use it."

"What's the last image in your head from last night?" Loke asked. He was still mostly focused on gathering the pages together, but he was not asking as casually as he wanted it to sound.

I closed my eyes and cast my mind back. "I was thinking about how it's impossible to really draw the wind," I said. "And then I had a sudden insight. I knew how to do it. How I wish I could remember what that epiphany was now."

"Maybe it's on one of these papers?" Roarr said hopefully.

"Doubtful. Pretty sure that's impossible," Loke said.

"Yeah," I agreed. "But for a second there, I thought I had it. Then I remember feeling like a wind was blowing through me, through my body and my mind both. And then I was waking up over there just a minute ago."

"Sounds like divine inspiration," Loke said, looking down at the pages in his hands. "Too bad this all looks like a total mess. Next time, try to dial it back a little."

"It's not all a mess," Roarr said, holding up a large sheet of newsprint so that Loke and I could both see it. "This looks like Báfurr is patrolling. And here's Villmark in the hills in the background."

"And he's walking away from it, with no intention of returning," Loke said dryly. "You're right. That tracks."

"Báfurr left town?" I asked.

"He didn't come back from patrol," Loke said.

"He told his partner he was going to head out towards where he thinks the Thors might be and volunteer for their mission," Roarr said.

"Who knows where that might be?" I said miserably.

"Well, apparently, you do," Loke said, and bent down to pick up a scrap of my fanciest paper, the kind I save for professional work only. Now it was covered in charcoal scribbles. But when Loke shuffled across the room to hand it to me, I saw it was indeed a sketch of Thorbjorn and Thorge, hiking through a mountain pass.

"This could be anywhere," I said.

"No, I know that place," Loke said. "And I'm pretty sure that you don't. It's very remote."

"It could be a coincidence," I said.

"Look, see how that jutting cliff looks like a face in profile? And this peak here looks like there's a bite taken out of it? That's the place. And if you don't believe me, ask Mjolner. He's clearly this smudgy thing in the tree down here."

I brought the page closer to my face to examine it. I wanted to deny it, but I couldn't. I knew that smudge of charcoal was Mjolner. I could clearly see where a few strokes of a kneaded eraser had defined the silver hammer that hung from his collar.

"So this is from the past, not from right now," I said.

"Because a cat who can walk through walls and teleport over great distances can't be in two places at once?" Loke teased. I looked up at him, startled at the thought. "I'm kidding. I'm pretty sure he can't. But I'm guessing if they aren't in this mountain pass now, they were there not too long ago."

"Is it bad, where they are?" I asked.

Maddeningly, Loke just shrugged. "It's in the wilds. Nothing out there is particularly *good*."

"Here's Báfurr again, in some kind of ruined village," Roarr said, bringing me another of the drawings. Mjolner was in this one too. But this one was overlaid by a thin pencil sketch of some entire other scene. I wasn't sure which of the two was meant to contain Mjolner. But I kind of thought he was in both.

"Here's another Mjolner," Loke said. "On his own in a tree."

"Mjolner, did you bring on the wind?" I whispered to him. He uncurled from my lap enough to look up at me and give me a slow wink. Then he tucked his head back in under his arm and went back to sleep.

"There's someone else in this one with Mjolner in a bog," Roarr said, squinting at the page in his hands. "I don't know this guy."

"Let me see," I said, and he handed it to me. I knew that hat at once, even in the blacks and whites of a pencil sketch. "That's Leifr. But I don't recognize where he is."

"This is the same bog, but a little kid this time," Roarr said, handing me another.

"Leifr again," I said. "And you, Mjolner. You really get around, don't you?"

The cat ignored me, and Roarr had gone back to sorting through the pages nearer the fireplace.

"Do you see any more with the Thors in it?" I asked, looking around at everything within my reach.

"No, but I'm sorting them into separate piles. This is Leifr again?" Roarr asked, showing me another drawing. I squinted at it, then nodded.

I looked at the drawing of Thorbjorn and Thorge on the mountain pass. Despite the harsh, dark lines I had used to draw the scene, I felt no menace in it. They were just walking through a stark landscape, nothing more.

"I suppose I should study all the ones with Báfurr in them first, if we're going to figure out where to find him," I said.

"You aren't going to just let him go like you did with Solvi?" he asked.

"Solvi stood in judgment first," I said. "Báfurr hasn't yet."

"Because if he was really trying to get to the Thors to help with their mission, that's doing a service for all of Villmark," Roarr said. "Maybe it would be okay to let him go."

"Yes, but if he was lying about that to get away from his patrol buddy, then he's fleeing justice," I said. "I have to talk to him to know which is which. And even then, I think he should stand before the council first and go help the Thors after."

"Getting this sorted isn't going to be a quick or easy job," Roarr admitted. He had a stack of loose pages in each hand, and sizable piles forming at his feet. But it didn't take more than the most cursory of glances around the room to know he had barely scratched the surface.

But suddenly I was aware of the fact that not only had Loke stopped contributing to the conversation, he seemed to be very busy doing something behind my back.

I turned around to see him shoving page after page from the floor around my easel into a sack. And not neatly. He was scrunching and tearing the pages in his hurry.

I encouraged Mjolner to get off my lap, then crossed the room to snatch the latest sheet of paper out of Loke's hand.

"This is you," I said, although it took me a moment to recognize it. This corner had more charcoal than pencil drawing, and the overlapping layers were dense. Still, I would recognize Loke's posture anywhere.

Then I looked more closely at every other drawing around me. I took the sack from his hands. He tried to hold on to it and not let me have it, but only for a second. Then he let go and stepped back, defeated.

"These are all you," I said. I had drawn Loke in Runde, in Villmark, in the same abandoned village I had drawn Báfurr in, in the mountain pass the Thors had passed through, in the dwarven city under the mountain I had once visited. I had even drawn him in my childhood home in St. Paul.

"Why are you everywhere?" I asked as I dug through page after page of Loke, dressed all in black, slouching through every place I had ever been.

I looked up at the real Loke, live and in the flesh in my own living room. He took a breath as if about to speak, to tell all, to finally unburden his soul.

But then he let the breath out again with a little shake of his head and took half a step back from me.

"Roarr, why don't you let the sorting go for now?" I said. "There's no food in this house, and going after Báfurr is definitely going to involve a hike. Can you go bring back some breakfast? And coffee. Lots of coffee."

Roarr looked at me in surprise. Then he looked at Loke, who was staring down at his own feet.

"Yeah. I can do that, Ingrid," Roarr said. Rather than just dropping what he had in his hands, he looked at each and set it in its assigned pile. Then he gave me a nod of farewell and headed out into the spring morning. The sounds of people passing in the street in front of my house filled the living room for the brief moment when the door was open.

Then it slammed shut again, and we were once more in silence, save for the soft purr of Mjolner's napping breath.

Now was the time. Loke was going to tell me everything.

Or as much of everything as would fit in the few minutes Roarr would be gone.

CHAPTER SEVENTEEN

THE ENTIRE SOUTH wall of my Villmark house was nothing but windows, offering a view of the lower half of the village and the hills beyond and letting in the maximum amount of winter sun. While the interior was not all white like Signi's house, the wood paneling and furniture were still light in color, and reflected and amplified the sunlight as the sun rose high enough in the east to flood in through the windows.

I had chosen the northwest corner of the room to set up my drawing area because it got the least direct sunlight. And that was where Loke was standing now, in the only shadow that still remained. His black clothes and chocolate brown hair were like camouflage in those shadows, but his pale face shone like a sickly moon.

He had stepped back against the wall, crushing papers under his feet, and he was studiously not looking at me.

I turned to find my art bag half under the still-napping Mjolner and pulled out my wand. Then I waved it in the air before my eyes as I looked at Loke.

"Hey, stop that," he objected at once, then advanced toward me when I made no move to do as he asked.

I wasn't sure what I had expected to see. Something like Odd, perhaps, filled with a magic completely unlike mine or my grandmother's. Or something like Leifr, carrying the remains of spells that had been cast over him.

Both of those things were there, but they were hard to see. It was like he glowed with a strange dark light all his own, but like nothing I had ever seen.

"Stop it, Ingrid," he said, as he finally got close enough to catch my wrist and force my hand down. "You don't want to mess with this."

"You were about to tell me something. I know you were," I said.

"It would be a mistake to tell you. I can't do it," he said.

"I think half of that is true," I said. Then I slinked my wrist out of his grasp and stepped back, wand raised once more.

I had seen something, like a magical gag tied around his mouth. If someone had used magic to command him to silence, it would explain why he kept not telling me things, even though I could tell he wanted to. He kept saying it wasn't the right time, but those words had become less and less convincing over time.

But the idea that something was keeping him from just telling me? That I found very believable.

"Mjolner, can you help?" I asked my cat. He looked up at me, then at Loke.

"That's really not a good idea," Loke said, backing away from both of us. But Mjolner was too fast for him. Without the slightest hint of sleepiness to him, the cat dashed across the room and lept up into Loke's arms. Loke, by reflex, caught him, but before he could set him down again Mjolner was biting down on his cheek.

Loke shrieked, and I began to doubt my plan. What was Mjolner doing to him? Besides drawing a lot of blood in that way that cats could do, suddenly and with no warning.

Then Mjolner yelped and jumped away, disappearing up the stairs towards the bedrooms.

"Ingy!" Loke said indignantly, pressing the back of his sleeve to his bleeding face.

"Sorry. I thought you were under some sort of silencing spell. I really thought that would help," I said. "I'll get a first aid kit. You should wash those cuts out with alcohol right away."

"I *was* under a spell, Ingrid," he said. He looked at the blood on his sleeve and rotated his arm to press a clean patch back to his mouth.

"Seriously?" I asked.

"Yes. But I still meant what I said. You can't mess with this. You're not ready."

"Halldis?" I asked. It felt like a cold hand was slowly closing over my heart. But I didn't feel much relief when he shook his head at me.

"Worse," he said.

"Tell me what you can, then," I said. "But come upstairs first. I want to clean those wounds before they get infected."

"I'm sure I'm fine," he said, but let me pull him up the stairs to the bathroom. There was no sign of Mjolner in any of the bedrooms we passed, but he was probably in my own room at the end of the hall, sprawling out on my bed all by himself.

Loke waited until I had swabbed every bite and scratch with copious amounts of alcohol, hissing only a little at the sting. But he refused to let me bandage anything, preferring instead to just hold gauze to it and wait for the bleeding to stop.

"It was a spell keeping you from telling me things," I said.

"Yes," he said. "Not just you. But it felt stronger around you. Probably because you're the one I really wanted to talk to about it."

"And you still won't tell me who did this? Or can't?" I asked.

"Won't," he said firmly. "It's not relevant at the moment, so just let it go."

"What *is* relevant?" I asked.

"I suppose the part that's gotten worse since you came to town," he said. Then he took another deep breath, only this time he didn't just release it. This time, he started to talk. "I can move across long distances in an instant. All those places you drew me in, I was there at some point in the last few months."

"Handy power," I said.

"It's not in my control," he said. "I just end up in some place I never meant to go, and I have to try to figure out why I'm there."

"There's a reason?" I asked.

"Either that, or I find a reason to justify what's happening to myself," he said almost bitterly. "It's out of control, and it's interfering with my most important job. Looking out for my sister."

"You get pulled out of your house?" I asked.

"All the time," he said. "Why do you think I'm never dressed for the weather? Because I never go out through my front door. I just turn up, unprepared, in some place I never intended to go."

"I've specifically asked you about the coat thing," I said.

"I know," he said, and gestured at the cuts on his face. "I'm telling you why now."

"So this started when I got in town?" I asked.

"No, I've been doing it since I was a kid. It's just gotten way more frequent and completely out of control since you were in town," he said.

"You think I triggered something?" I asked.

He just shrugged and leaned into the mirror to assess the damage.

"Or maybe—" I said, but then trailed off, not sure I should speak my thoughts out loud.

"Tell me," Loke said. "Whatever you're thinking."

I sighed. "My grandmother admitted to me once that she pulls power out of you to maintain the spells at the mead hall," I said.

"No way," he said. "No, I would know… wouldn't I?"

"I'm not sure you would," I said. "She started after my mother left town, but stopped when I came home last year."

Loke looked skeptical, but the more I thought about it, the more sense it made.

"She said your power was chaotic, almost uncontrollable," I said. He just shrugged. "But if she was taking a little of that chaos away from you, small amounts over time, maybe it was like a pressure valve to you. It kept you from accumulating too much. But now that she isn't—" I broke off, but now he was nodding a half-hearted agreement.

"Maybe," he said. "Maybe."

"We should talk to my grandmother about this," I said. "Especially about your involuntary trips and about the spell I just removed."

"Not now," Loke said wearily. "I don't want to pull Nora into this any more than I want to see you pulled into it."

"Into what, exactly?" I asked.

But he just shook his head. "I made a mess of some things, but it's a mess that's on me to clean up. Don't worry; it's not something that's too much for me to deal with. But now isn't the time."

"At the very least, you should talk to my grandmother about siphoning off your power again," I said. "Just so you can regain control."

"That I'll do for sure, now that I know she was even doing that before," he said. "For now, we need to deal with the Báfurr situation, and then the Thors situation."

As if summoned by those words, I heard Roarr coming in through my front door below. We headed downstairs, lured by the rich smell of fresh coffee and cinnamon rolls.

Then the three of us tackled every scrap of paper that was piled up in the living room. We ended up with four piles: pictures of Báfurr, pictures of Leifr, pictures of the Thors, and pictures of—as far as we could tell—nothing at all.

The piles were not remotely of equal size. The pictures of nothing far outnumbered the other three. And there was only the single image of the Thors in the mountain pass, no more.

The Leifr pictures formed a sort of circle of the same bog, forest, and meadow, but each with a slightly older Leifr somewhere in the image. I set those aside to dwell on later.

"Mostly you've drawn him in this abandoned village," Roarr said as he drained the last of his coffee.

"Do you know it?" I asked as casually as I could. I had already said the name of Halldis aloud once that morning. I didn't want to repeat it, especially not to Roarr. I had been in her magical thrall for a short time, but he had lived in it for days and days. I'm sure it wasn't a memory he ever wanted to revisit.

But he just picked up one of the drawings and examined it more closely, then set it aside to reach for his fourth cinnamon roll. "No. Never been there. It's not where I got that amulet, if that's what you're thinking. That place was barely the remains of a campsite. Definitely not a village like this."

Loke smirked but said nothing.

"You said you knew where this was?" I said to him.

"I can get you there," he said, still grinning.

"What about me?" Roarr asked.

"I need you to go to Frór's cabin and talk to my grandmother. Catch her up on what we're doing," I said. "I'm not making an excuse to send you away. This is important, that she knows."

"Of course," Roarr said, but I could see him working to hide his disappointment.

"Talk to the council first, though. Find out what they're planning to do with Odd's body. My grandmother will want to know," I said. He nodded.

"She'll want to know, but she'll stuff you with waffles at the same time," Loke said.

"I have no problem with that," Roarr said. "What about Kara and Nilda? They told me you were going to see them before you left Villmark."

"I will. Loke and I are just running out and back again. Once we have Báfurr, we're bringing him here," I said.

"This village is close?" Roarr asked, frowning at the mountains that were dark smudges in the background of every drawing. Very tall dark smudges.

"It is for me," Loke said.

"I will be back in Villmark before dinnertime," Roarr said as he got up to go. "I'll come back here?"

"Perfect, but no hurry," I said, then walked him to the door.

Loke just lingered in the hallway, waiting for Roarr to go. I turned to him once I'd shut the door. "This is a planned trip. You should have a coat," I said.

"My house is in the exact opposite direction. I'll be fine. My chaos keeps me warm," he added with a wicked smile.

"Yeah, but wear a coat anyway," I said. I opened the lid of the bench under the hooks in my mudroom and found an old cloak. Perhaps it had been my great-grandfather's. Perhaps it was even older than that. But it was thick wool trimmed in fur, deliciously warm, and only faintly musty.

Plus, it was all in black. I handed it to Loke, and he rolled his eyes but put it on.

I shoved a hat and gloves at him too, then shut the bench lid and reached for my own things.

"Are we taking the north road or the west road out of town?" I asked as I tucked my hair under my hat.

"If this works, neither," Loke said.

"If what works?" I asked, but he just motioned for me to step aside.

I moved back to let him go out the door first. He grasped the doorknob tightly, but he didn't turn it right away. He just stood there, looking for all the world like he was trying to get up the nerve to enter my front garden.

Then he turned the knob and flung the door open with a flourish. A grin slowly spread across his face.

The full light of the sun was on him, which immediately struck me as wrong. It was too late in the morning for it to be hitting him at that angle.

Then I realized all the street noise was gone. No rattling of cartwheels on the cobblestones, no chattering of people heading south to the market or north to the center of the village.

I had to get up on tiptoes to see over his shoulder.

Spread out outside my door was the living version of my pencil and charcoal drawings, the abandoned village in the foothills under the mountains between Villmark and Old Norway.

I had seen a lot of magic since coming home to Runde, but nothing like this.

We stepped through the door.

CHAPTER EIGHTEEN

THE MINUTE I was on the other side, I turned back around to see what we had just walked out of.

It was the charred remains of a doorway in a hut that had partly burned to the ground. The back and right walls were mostly gone, but the front and left side were still standing, supporting what they could of the sagging remains of the roof.

But inside that doorway, I was looking at my own front hall.

"You can do this whenever you want?" I asked, sticking my hand through the doorway. It didn't feel any different on one side or the other. There was no buzz of magic or anything. It was warmer in my hall, but that was all.

And yet, I knew everything beyond my right wrist was now many miles away from where my feet were standing.

It was a creepy thought.

"I don't have much control," Loke admitted. "I just had a feeling it would work this time. Something in the air of your house just felt... orderly."

"My rune magic," I guessed. "I was meditating on a rune that represents order."

"You generated a lot of chaos doing that," Loke pointed out.

"But you felt order," I countered.

Then I turned my attention back to the doorway, and the charred remains of a door hanging from a single hinge.

"Should we block this somehow? If it closes, are we trapped here, or can you do that trick again?" I asked.

"I don't know what will happen when I try again, but I promise you, blocking the door never works," he said. He sounded infinitely tired. I was sure he had tried everything to control his power over the last few months.

"What happens?" I asked.

"When I turn away from the door, it goes back to its normal state," he said. "Watch." He walked across the open space between where we were standing and the next half-burned cottage, then turned back again. He waved towards the door beside me and I turned to see the doorway behind me no longer led back to my home. It only led into the burnt remains of someone else's home, long abandoned.

"So we're stuck here?" I asked.

"Villmark is a long walk in that direction," Loke said with a vague wave to the southeast. "If worse comes to worse. But first we should find Báfurr."

"The sketches didn't really give a sense of time," I said as we looked around.

"No, but we know he left Villmark last night. I would guess he got here at sunrise if he walked all night. Maybe a little later," Loke said.

I really hoped his trick would work twice, and we could take the shortcut home. Otherwise, it sounded like a lot of walking.

"Who lived here?" I wondered.

"People have walked away from Villmark before," Loke said as he bent to pick up a very tarnished spoon half buried in the mud. "But somehow I don't think these were Villmarkers."

"Why not?" I asked, taking the spoon from him to examine it myself. It was very rudimentary, like something from the Middle Ages. But nowhere near that old.

"I've been to other villages in the wilds," he said softly. "The people there weren't Villmarkers."

"Who were they?" I asked and found myself whispering too. As if the charred remains of houses were trying to listen in.

"Just people," he said. "But places like this, abandoned places? Other things move in."

"Like what?" I asked.

"Like *not* people," he said. We had reached what seemed to be the center of the village. Like Villmark, this was an open square with a well in the center. The last of the ice from the rainstorm had melted away, leaving nothing but tall brown grass and lots of mud.

But that grass was bent and broken. And the mud was freshly churned up.

"There was a fight here," Loke said as he walked slowly around the square, bent over as he examined the ground. He stopped and pointed out a print to me. "Boots. Could be from Báfurr."

"And that?" I asked, pointing to an enormous mark that dominated a clear patch of ground near the stone wall of the well. "Is that from a bear?"

"Bear? No," Loke said, turning to look at the print from a different angle. "A paw print from a bear would have five round toes across the top in a line. This has only four."

I saw he was right. There were markings of two toes in the front and one on each side set a little behind the front two, a tapered print. "What is it, then?" I asked.

He pushed the hood of his cloak back from his face and scanned the edge of the forest all around us, just beyond the burned huts. "Wolf," he said at last.

"Wolf? This print is nearly a foot across," I said. "No wolf is that big."

"That's not what's worrying me," Loke said, still looking around, but this time scanning the ground.

"What's worrying you?" I asked. Giant wolves were certainly enough to put me on high alert.

"I can see where this wolf goes," he said, pointing out the line of tracks that led away from the well. Then he turned to point at the ground behind him. "But not where it came from."

"Did it come out of the well?" I asked. I screwed up my courage and moved close enough to peer over the side of the well.

But there was nothing down there. I could see where the water level was, not too far down. And the top was iced over. A dried leaf and little bits of dry grass were caught inside that ice, but there was no sign of animal prints on its surface.

"I'm not liking this," Loke said. "Something doesn't feel right."

I took out my wand and waved it before my eyes. I saw no signs of spells around us, not even at the doorway we had just stepped through.

But the ground through the waving of the wand looked strange. Like it was covered with bird scratches all over in an intricate fanlike pattern.

"The Wild Hunt," I said under my breath.

"What?" Loke asked, swallowing nervously.

I stopped moving the wand, and the ground was once more dried grass and mud, if freshly disturbed. No sign of bird scratches or feathery patterns.

"I thought I saw the signs of the Wild Hunt passing through here," I said.

"But that summoning amulet is gone," Loke said. "And it's the wrong time of year for the Wild Hunt. Far too sunny, far too much daytime."

"I know," I said as I tucked my wand away.

"What sign is it that you see?" he asked, still sounding incredibly nervous. Which did my own nerves no good at all.

"It's like birds were here," I said. "Have you ever seen the mark on the snow where an owl swooped down and grabbed a mouse or something? The pattern their wings make? It's like that, only without the mouse imprint."

"There's no snow here," Loke pointed out.

"No, but I see the same kind of bird pattern," I said.

"Maybe it's not the Wild Hunt per se but some other aspect of Odin," Loke said.

"Why?" I asked. He just shrugged.

"Because Odd died, maybe? I don't know. You know most of the time I'm just guessing, right?" he said with a grin.

"But you know most of the time your guesses turn out to be right, *right*?" I countered.

He just shrugged. Then he straightened as something caught his eye. "Ingrid," he said, walking carefully around the wolf paw prints to a bent blade of grass. "Blood."

"Human or wolf?" I asked.

"I don't know," he said, looking up from the blade of grass towards the forest beyond.

I looked at the drops already dried on the blade. "It's mostly dry but not brown yet," I said. "Still rather fresh, wouldn't you say?"

"They went this way," Loke said, and started down the path that led out of the village.

He had a knife in each hand. I don't know where he got them from. His leggings and tunic wouldn't have hidden them before, and I know they weren't in the cloak when I handed it to him. And yet there they were, gleaming in his hands.

I took my wand back out, for all the good it would do me, and followed him.

The ground in the village had been frozen hard, but in the forest it was squishier. The air was also warmer, but not uniformly. It was like there were warm pockets we kept passing through. And those pockets had a loamy smell that was offputting.

Then I stepped in the squishiest bit of all, my foot sucking down past my ankle. Loke had to double back to pull me free. I just barely kept my boot, mostly thanks to the tightness of my laces and my double knots. But pulling it free released a cloyingly thick smell worse than anything I'd ever smelled before.

And I had visited a pig farm in the second grade.

Loke had a finger pressed to his lips to remind me we were being quiet. I was pretty sure I hadn't yelped out loud, but it took a bit of work to keep my dry heaves silent.

Then I heard a rumbling growl, and the sound of overly large paws slapping down on the wet ground.

Loke and I followed the sound until we could make out snowy white fur from among the gray trunks of early spring trees. The growling was louder now, suddenly pitching up to an aggressive snarl. Then there was a clang of metal on stone and the snarl settled back into a patient growl.

I clutched my wand tightly, but it gave me no comfort. I knew absolutely no spells that would drive off a monstrously huge wolf. It had to be twice the size of a polar bear.

And I really hoped it was alone. Because if this wolf had a pack, we were walking into deep trouble for sure.

Loke motioned for me to stay back, then took another dozen or so steps closer to the wolf. The wolf had its back to us, bending over to torment something that seemed to be wedged between a fallen tree and the rocky side of an eroded hill. Loke took a few more steps, silently moving the shoulders of his cloak back out of his way. Then he raised one of those gleaming knives and hurled it straight at the wolf.

It hit the wolf square between the shoulder blades, burying itself all the way to the hilt. A gush of red blood ran from the wound, staining the white fur.

Then the wolf rose up. I hadn't realized it had been stooped over before. It had certainly seemed tall enough. But now it was standing at its full height and towering over the dark form of Loke.

It was three times his height and many, many times his width.

But he didn't fall back. He just switched the other knife over to his right hand and took aim with it.

The wolf loomed over him, its snarling mouth open as if to snatch his entire body up off the ground. Spittle dripped from its massive teeth, and its breath was blowing back the locks of Loke's hair.

Then its body seized up, throwing its head back as it cried out in pain, but from no blow I could see. The second knife was still in Loke's hand. But the wolf shrieked and spun back around, then shrieked a third time before falling to the ground with a rush of exhaled air.

"Loke?" I called.

"It's all right, Ingrid," he called back to me, although I noticed he hadn't lowered that knife yet.

"What happened?" I asked as I crept forward. It certainly looked dead. Its eyes were rolled back and its tongue was lolled out of its mouth, not moving.

"Báfurr happened," Loke said. Then he finally put his knife away and stepped aside just as Báfurr on the far side of the mountain of wolf lowered his own blood-drenched sword.

Never in my life had expected to see that look on Báfurr's face, but there was no doubt about it.

He was legitimately happy to see me.

CHAPTER NINETEEN

Báfurr may have slain that mountain-sized white wolf, but the wolf had gotten some licks in first. Báfurr was holding his sword in both hands, and even after he lowered the blade, I could still see it tremble in his unsteady grasp. Blood from a head wound covered half his face and coated his beard, and his torso was soaked from a large bite that encompassed his entire left shoulder. And when he stepped towards Loke, he was dragging one foot behind him.

"I killed it," he said disbelievingly, staring down at the wolf's gaping maw. "I didn't think I could. I didn't think it was even possible."

"It's monstrously huge, sure, but mortal for all that," Loke said, giving the corpse a disrespectful kick.

"You don't understand, this thing fell out of the sky," Báfurr said in a harsh whisper, looking up at the clouds overhead as if he feared something else was about to come down and kill us.

"Did you disturb something in that village? Some artifact or something?" Loke asked.

"No!" Báfurr said. "I don't know why it appeared there. I felt it stalking me all the way from Villmark. It's why I left Manni behind. I knew it was coming for me, and I didn't want him hurt."

"The two of you could've taken it," Loke said. "Manni is a better fighter than I am, surely."

I looked at the wolf's body between them through the waving of my wand and saw once more the bird-wing patterns all over the ground. They seemed to spread out from the body like ripples around where a rock fell in a pond.

"If it followed you from Villmark, then it didn't fall from the sky," I said. "But it is infused with magic. I can see that clearly. Perhaps in addition to its larger than normal size, it can jump so high it looks like to comes down from nowhere."

"I won't argue with you," Báfurr said, almost as if he were admonishing himself.

"Why did you think it was hunting you?" I asked as I came closer to look at the wolf. Now that it wasn't snarling and baring its fangs, it struck me as a rather beautiful animal. Its fur was so thick and snowy white, if it had been a dog I wouldn't have been able to resist cuddling it.

"I felt it stalking me, like I said, all the way from Villmark," Báfurr said. "Clearly Odin sent it. Because of what I did."

"I think it's more likely just a lost creature from the northern wilds," I said. "Lost far from Old Norway. It's the simpler explanation."

But even as I spoke, the creature started to sparkle like snow in bright sunlight. The sparkle intensified to a blinding light and then flashed away all at once, leaving nothing but a twinkling of snow that settled back down to the ground in the perfect outline of the wolf's body. Loke's knife remained in the center of the form, and he bent down to pick it up.

"Or not," I said.

"You think Odin is looking to punish you for what you did to Odd, then?" Loke asked. He was cleaning his knives with a scrap of cloth. Then, with a swirl of his cloak, knives and cloth both disappeared from view.

"I know he is," Báfurr said grimly, and I forced my attention away from whatever magic Loke was doing to focus on him.

"The way Raggi told us the story, it sounded like it was at least in part an accident," I said.

"I pushed him. There's no talking my way around that fact," Báfurr said. Then he took out a rag of his own to clean his sword before sliding it back into its scabbard at his waist. His hands were still trembling, and his complexion was pale to the point of looking ashen.

"You need to get back to Villmark," I said. "You need a healer."

"I'm fine," he said dismissively.

"You know that you have to face this," Loke said to him. "If this wolf assassin was indeed sent by Odin, he won't be the last. Until you make restitution, there will be no rest for you."

"Don't you think I know it?" Báfurr said with a fierce grief.

"You can't keep running from it," I said. "You need to face the council. But tell them your tale. I know they will listen to you with mercy and fairness. What you did was serious, and the consequences must match it. But running away isn't going to help."

"That wolf won't be the last," Loke said again.

"So I must spend the rest of my days in a dank cell in the caves behind the waterfall?" Báfurr asked bitterly.

"If that's what is required," I said. "But I don't think that will be your fate. I know I'm new to Villmark, but I've spent a lot of that little time with the council. I know some of how they think. The only criminals placed in those cells are those who are still and will always remain a danger to others. Do you think that describes you? Or can you make amends and start anew?"

"Like Roarr?" Báfurr asked.

"Roarr never actually killed anyone," Loke said.

"But he's worked hard to make amends for what he *did* do ever since," I said. "There is a path before you that offers you similar hope. But you have to admit to what you did. In every detail."

"I didn't think he could die," Báfurr said, looking at the ground at his feet and speaking low, as if to himself. "I never thought he could actually die. But that's no excuse. I let my anger take me. Only for an instant, but that instant was enough."

Then he fell silent. Finally, I felt compelled to speak. "Will you come back with us to stand before the council?" I asked.

"Yes. I will," he agreed. "Do you want to take my arms?"

"No, you carry them," Loke said. "No sense weighing Ingrid or I down, as I'm sure you intend us no harm."

"No, I do not," Báfurr said.

"And just in case another wolf does come, they might come in handy," Loke said.

"You can hide us from the sight of such creatures, can you not?" Báfurr asked me.

"I think so," I said, and quickly worked the few concealment spells I knew. It was strange doing them without my grandmother, but it felt like I had cast them correctly. "That should do it," I said when I had finished and put my wand away again.

"So you're going to throw yourself at the mercy of the council," Loke said to Báfurr with a grin. "The very council you were meeting with Odd in the hopes of overthrowing. Ironic."

"Yes, that is exactly what I'm doing," Báfurr said a tad defensively. "A lot has changed in the last few days."

"The wolf?" Loke asked.

"No, before that," Báfurr said. "I've had a lot of time to think. It's pretty much all I've been doing since it happened. Even when I was out on patrol."

He gave us both a long look, then started trudging back towards the village, limping and dragging his leg behind him. There was no way we were walking all the way back to Villmark. At his pace it would take days.

But even when that problem should've been paramount in my mind, I found myself looking to the north. We were far north of Villmark, and yet the mountains on the horizon looked no closer. Just how far away were Thorbjorn and Thorge?

And what might be pursuing them? Was it a wolf like the one we had just slain?

A shiver went up my spine. Maybe Báfurr was wrong. Maybe that wolf had been pursuing him because he was on patrol outside the village perimeter and not because of what he had done.

Things were awakening and stirring. That was why the Thors had left in the first place, as well as Frór. Maybe this wolf was part of that.

"What are you thinking?" Loke asked me.

"I'm thinking I need to talk to my grandmother about casting spells of protection around Villmark. I mean newer, more targeted ones than the ones Torfa put over everything," I said. "I think the patrols might be in danger."

"Good thought," Loke said, but he looked surprised.

"What?" I asked.

"I just thought you were looking to the north because you were considering walking that way," he said with a shrug.

"I worry about them," I admitted. "Kara felt like they were being pursued by some monster she couldn't see."

"You think maybe like that wolf?" Loke asked, looking back at the already-melting snow.

"Maybe," I said. "What do you think?"

"I don't know," he admitted. "Until you mentioned it, I was pretty sure that Báfurr was right. Maybe not that the wolf was sent by Odin himself. But certainly killing Odd upset a lot of things. We don't really know where or how deep he traveled all the years he was away from Villmark. Where he made allies, and where he made enemies. And if those are also our allies and enemies or something else."

"We have to get back to Villmark," I said. "Can you do your trick again? Or is Báfurr's presence likely to ruin things?"

"I won't really know until I try," he said.

We quickly caught up with Báfurr, then walked with him to the hovel where we had entered the village.

"Why are we stopping?" Báfurr asked grumpily. He was clearly in pain, and even more clearly not going to say so. I could empathize with him that it was easier to maintain his slow gait than to stop and start again.

"Loke might have a shortcut," I said.

"Some kind of tunnel?" Báfurr asked skeptically. He gazed off at the forested hills that stood between us and Villmark.

"Better," Loke promised him. Then he placed his hands on the handle of the remains of the charred door. Once again, he just stood grasping it for a long moment as he built up his courage or focus or whatever. Then he turned the handle and slowly swung the door outward.

Once more, I could see my own front hall. It had never looked so good. I put an arm around Báfurr and helped him over the threshold. Loke came in behind us and shut the door with a bang, as if he wanted to be sure no pathway to my house remained.

I certainly appreciated that, although I wasn't sure if the loud slam were necessary. Still, better safe than sorry.

I didn't think Mjolner would take to any canine visitors, particularly not of the giant white wolf variety.

"I'll fetch a healer and let everyone know Báfurr is back," Loke said. Then he added to me, "if you feel safe staying here alone with him?"

"Perfectly safe," I assured him. "But hurry. He's bleeding all over my hallway floor."

"Sorry," Báfurr mumbled, and unclasped his cloak to stand and drip on that.

"I'll hurry," Loke promised us both, then turned back to my front door. He opened it onto a view of my front garden and the street beyond, then sprinted away.

"If you wanted to judge me as volva, I would accept that readily," Báfurr said to me. "Nora used to do such things in this house. It's pretty much all she did in this house."

"Thank you for that. I appreciate what it means, and I take it to heart," I said. "But this house is just a house now. And especially in this matter, I don't want to usurp the council."

"You'll never be one of us, not deep down, not really," he said, and my heart sank at his words. But then he went on, "but I'm starting to see the value of you, who you are. You are worthy to stand among us, foreigner though you may be."

"Thank you, Báfurr," I said with a sigh, and really hoped he wasn't going to feel the need to keep talking the entire time we were alone together.

Loke couldn't return fast enough for me.

CHAPTER TWENTY

LESS THAN AN HOUR LATER, I was once again alone in my quiet little house. The noonday sun was shining in brightly through all the windows, illuminating all of my artwork in its separate piles, as well as the streaks of charcoal and graphite that marred the wood floor everywhere I looked.

I had a lot of work ahead of me, cleaning all that up.

But my brain was muffled like cotton, like I couldn't hear my own thoughts. Loke had rattled off a list of things he'd done or would be doing when he'd returned to put Báfurr in a cart to roll him to the healer's house. But my tired brain hadn't been able to follow his rapid-fire speech well enough to even grasp if there was something I should be doing.

Besides cleaning up the mess I'd made of my living room floor. I should really get started on that.

But instead, I headed upstairs to my bedroom. Mjolner was already there, curled up on the pillow of my bed. He didn't stir or open his eyes, only mewed softly as I slumped down onto the bed beside him and fell into a sudden, deep sleep.

When I woke it was early evening, the sun having just slipped out of sight behind the hills to the west. I'm sure the sudden chill that accompanied that moment was what had woken me.

Mjolner was gone wherever it was that Mjolner went. Given what I had drawn the night before, that could pretty much be everywhere. If I drew him now in a Parisian café, I wouldn't be surprised to find out it was true.

I got up and headed downstairs, hoping that Roarr had left something like food or, better yet, coffee in my kitchen that morning. But I was only halfway down the stairs when I heard a knock at my front door. I quickened my pace to open the door and let Loke in.

He was holding a basket covered with a folded kitchen towel, but the smells coming out from under that towel were divine.

"From the Mikkelsen sisters," he said. "They just threw together a bunch of sandwiches, as they do."

"Just threw together the world's greatest sandwiches," I agreed as we headed to the kitchen together and I put on a kettle for tea.

"I came with food, but also with news," Loke said as we unpacked the basket together. The sandwiches were roast beef with stone-ground mustard on dark bread filled with caraway seeds, and they were still warm.

"News?" I said around a mouth full of sandwich. I would've been more embarrassed if I hadn't been so very hungry.

"Báfurr felt well enough to go before the council the minute he was patched up," Loke said. "I mean, he still looked terrible, but I think he was anxious to get it over with. Wolf fear."

"I think he wants to be at peace with himself, and that's the first step to doing that," I said, but Loke just rolled his eyes at me. "What was their verdict?"

"I guess you'd think of it like house arrest, or maybe like halfway house? Anyway, he's moving in with Gunna and Valki. They will be watching over him when he's not on patrol. But mostly he'll be out on patrol. Doing service for the community."

"For how long?" I asked.

Loke shrugged. "Until they think he's proven himself, I guess.

Which will probably be sooner than he thinks that about himself. He's really self-flagellating at the moment."

"I think that's a good sign," I said. "Maybe he's being a bit excessive at the moment, but I'm sure that will calm down in time." Loke rolled his eyes at me again. "What, you don't think he's sincere?"

"Wolf fear," Loke said again, as if that explained everything. At my blank look, he went on, "I'm sure in his own mind he's quite sincere. I'm equally sure when the wolves don't come after him again, that he'll starting feeling and thinking differently. He's going to forget some of the things he's been swearing to today."

"Maybe," I said. "But maybe not. Maybe he really is coming around. And if he's going on patrol with the others, maybe he can get them asking the right sorts of questions too."

"Now you've gone too far," Loke said, jabbing an accusatorial finger at me. "Not even you can be that optimistic. No, that's not the word. What is the word I'm thinking of? Oh, yes. Naïve."

"So Báfurr is the only one who's been out on patrol who's felt like they were being stalked?" I asked.

"I don't actually know that," Loke admitted. "We can talk to Valki about it, I suppose."

"And I need to talk to Nilda and Kara," I said. "But I might have to come back into town for that. I really think I need to start with talking to my grandmother about those protection spells."

"I'm inclined to agree with you," Loke said.

"You should come with me," I said, then put the last bite of my sandwich in my mouth and wiped the mustard away with my napkin.

"No, thank you," Loke said.

"We already agreed we needed to talk to my grandmother about your powers," I said, once again around a mouth full of food. This time I couldn't plead hunger. That sandwich had been more than filling enough.

"I know," he sighed. "I was hoping to procrastinate about that more."

"Were you?" I laughed. "Of course you were." But then another thought struck me, and I quickly grew serious again. "If you needed to, could you get to the Thors in a hurry?"

"No," he said without even thinking about it.

"Are you sure?" I pressed.

"I move through doorways, Ingy," he said. "Actual, physical doorways. There are no doorways where they are."

"How do you know?" I asked, but not accusatorially. I was genuinely curious.

"I just do," he said, waving his hands in the air in vague gestures. "I feel it."

"You could at least get us a lot closer. You said there were more abandoned villages like the one Báfurr fought the wolf in," I said.

"I also told you those villages are largely haunted by things I want to tangle with even less than I want to face another wolf the size of a truck."

"What kinds of things?" I asked, shivering before he even said a word.

"Probably about what you're thinking," he said, watching me closely. "Draugr. Deildegaster. Gjenganger. Mylingar. Other undead creatures."

I could actually feel the color draining out of my cheeks. It left my face feeling cold. I pressed my palms to my cheeks to warm them.

Some of those things I had heard of before. Others were new to me. But I knew in my bones they were all bad news.

"Take heart," Loke said with more of his usual humor in his tone. "Whatever I know about these things, the Thors know in spades. I promise you, Thorbjorn and Thorge are steering well clear of the haunted spaces."

"Sticking to the wilds," I said. "And what is it that lurks there?"

"I'm not sure you want to know," he said. "In fact, I'm pretty certain you do not."

"They've been gone so long," I said.

"Their work isn't done yet," Loke said with a shrug, tossing the towel back into the now-empty basket. "If it makes you feel better, we both know that Mjolner can reach them anytime at all, anywhere they might be."

"But he's a tricky messenger," I said with a sigh. "I think he understands me when I speak, and sometimes I almost think he could answer back if he chose to. But mostly I think I'm probably kidding myself. Walking through walls is superpower enough, don't you think?"

"Superpowers," Loke scoffed. "No one can stop with just one."

I finished the last of my tea, then peeked out into my living room to see the sky already fading from deep purple to black.

"I'm too late to get to Frór's cabin now," I said with a sigh. "Maybe I *do* talk to Nilda and Kara first."

"Nonsense!" Loke said with a dramatic flourish of one arm. "Nilda and Kara can wait. You need to speak to your grandmother. So let's go, then." And he led me back to my own front door.

"If you don't mind, I'm getting my hat and jacket first and putting on my boots," I said.

"If you must," he said. "You'll be stepping out of this mudroom and into the other, but suit yourself."

"I'll be leaving that cabin at some point, and boots and a jacket will come in handy," I said. I put on all my layers and fetched my art bag from the living room. It was almost entirely empty, and I remembered I had never gotten around to cleaning up the living room.

Well, I had to be back soon anyway, to talk to Nilda and Kara. I would do it then.

"Ready?" Loke asked as I came back to the front door. He was standing with his hand on the doorknob, ready to turn it at any moment.

"Ready. Are you coming?" I asked.

"Not this time," he said. "I think it's better if you and Nora discuss me without me there, at least for the first time."

"You're cool with that?" I asked, surprised.

"I don't relish the thought, but I understand the necessity," he said. "Once you two figure out what you intend to do, send for me. Send

Mjolner. Whatever you might think about your own level of kidding yourself, I understand that cat perfectly fine."

"It certainly seems like you do," I allowed. Then I clutched my art bag close to my belly and gave him a nod.

He summoned up his power then turned the doorknob. But when the door opened, what was on the far side wasn't the mudroom of Frór's cabin. But it *was* my bedroom door up in the loft.

And there on the bed, as if waiting for me, was Mjolner, curled up and napping.

"Did I mention my control isn't great?" Loke asked.

"I don't know. This seems close enough to me," I said. "But tell me this: until I asked you to, have you ever tried to deliberately go anywhere? Or do you just try to find reasons to be wherever you end up at random, like you said before?"

"I never had anywhere I wanted to go before," Loke said. "Not that I wouldn't prefer to reach on my own two feet, anyway. But as far as I can control it, my power will always be at your beck and call."

"Then I'm becking and calling for this," I said even as I stepped through the doorway to my bedroom on the shore of Lake Superior. "Practice. When I need to rely on you, I want you to be reliable."

"As you wish," he said with a little bow. Then he closed the door between us.

I opened it again and saw the hallway that stretched across the loft. I could smell meat cakes cooking in the kitchen and hear my grand-mother and Roarr speaking together, although too distantly to make out any words.

But mostly I felt the cabin around me, like it was hugging me in the way only a cozy little house could. The warmth and comfort of this special place I shared with my grandmother, the warmth and comfort that had been so violently destroyed by Odd's short visit, was back again.

And it was only the warmer for containing Roarr as well.

I ran down the stairs to the mudroom to put my things away. Everything that I needed to talk to my grandmother about would have to wait until Roarr was on his way, and that wouldn't be until after all those meat cakes were gone, but that was all right.

Because I felt spells all around me now, like I hadn't before. My grandmother had woven every protective spell she had ever shown me around the cabin, reinforcing its own magic.

She was definitely back at the top of her game.

Which was good. Because we had a lot of work to do.

CHAPTER TWENTY-ONE

THE NEXT WEDNESDAY morning was a warm spring day, the sky full of sunshine and even the wind off the lake not too unbearably cold. The meadows were still all brown, dead grass, but a few birds were calling to each other cheerily.

My grandmother and I stood at the very edge of the promontory between the back of the cabin and the straight fall down to the lake below. The council was with us. Valki looked worn out from all the extra patrol and guard work he had done around Villmark since his sons, the Thors, went north. Brigida was as coldly aloof as always, but she clutched the head of a sturdy walking stick in her beringed hands.

That was a new addition. It was like everyone in the council had aged years just in the few months I had known them.

And that included Haraldr, the oldest of the three. His eyes were bright, as alert as ever, and he seemed in good health, but there was no denying he was leaning more heavily on his staff than usual, even for him.

We were gathered around a stone cairn, having taken it in turns to place stones one by one over the body of Odd Oddsen. He had shrunken in death, all the hard muscle no more than sinew now, barely holding his bones together.

But now that we had finished, no one said a word or made a move to leave. For my part, I enjoyed the view all around us. And I was pretty sure that Odd would've approved of the location. His cairn could be seen far out to sea to the north and out over the waves of the lake to the south both. That would've meant something to him.

More important to me, the place where he had fallen wasn't visible from here. It wasn't so very far away, but with the cabin blocking the view, it felt distant enough not to be a reminder.

"I have met Odd three times in my lifetime," Valki said suddenly. "Once when I was a child, and I thought he was Odin himself come to life. The second time when I was a young man, and the words he spoke in the mead hall changed the path of my life from farmer to guardian of our people."

"And the third time?" I asked after a long moment of silence had elapsed.

"The third time was when I had just joined the council, turning my back on the life of a guardian always on patrol in favor of a life with my family in the village," he said. A darkness passed over his eyes, but he dispelled it with a shake of his head. "This isn't the time to speak of that meeting."

"I also met him three times," Brigida said. "As a child, I too was in awe of him. As a young woman, I felt something more like fear. Odin is meant to be a force of order and civilization, but Odd Oddsen felt like a force of disruption to me then. Even more so when I met him the third time. We traded words then. Let's leave it at that. But after he left town that time, I started the work that eventually put me on the council. I wanted to be sure that the council was as strong as I could make it before he came back to town."

We all fell silent again. I could hear voices from over the water, some atmospheric fluke bringing distant sounds to my ears over the crash of the waves below.

"I met Odd five times," Haraldr said at last. "When I was a boy, he told me stories, the sorts of stories that linger in your mind and shape you as you mature. The second time I was a teenager, and I followed him everywhere around town until he again told me stories, but darker, more twisted stories than the first time. Ones with hidden meanings, riddles for me to parse out over the years."

He shifted his weight from foot to foot, and I knew all this standing was hard on his old joints, but he just continued on with his story.

"The third time I was still a youth, but had no path. Everything I tried my hand at felt like the wrong use of my skills. He was the one who took me to the town library and showed me the oldest books. I spent years poring over those books, struggling with the old Norse words that had fallen out of use here in Villmark."

He shifted his weight again, leaning more on his staff, then went on. "The fourth time I was newly on the council. He wasn't pleased with my choice of using all the knowledge he had led me to in that way. He challenged me, both on my choice but also on my learning in general. I never knew if I passed that test in his eyes or not. He was always very hard to read."

"And the fifth time?" I asked.

"When he came back for the fifth time, I was the oldest member of the council, with Valki and the man who held the seat before Brigida. I don't remember his name," Haraldr said.

"Mats," Brigida said.

"That's right. Mats," Haraldr said. "He was a decent fellow. Died too soon." Then he looked down at the cairn, and we all shared the same unspoken thought, that the same couldn't be said of Odd Oddsen. Putting aside what any of us thought of him, he had lived a long, full life. Haraldr looked up and saw I was still waiting for him to finish the story, but he waved me off with a shaking hand. "Like Valki, I'm going to beg off telling that tale here and now. Some other day, perhaps."

"I won't count the number of times I met Odd Oddsen, for they are surely without number," my grandmother said. "He was a force of disruption, and sometimes that's needed. But disruption just for disruption's sake is not a good thing. And I was never sure that Odd Oddsen knew the difference." Then she huffed out a breath and turned away from the lake and the cairn both. "I have lunch ready inside. Let's go eat and leave this old crow to his slow decay."

As harsh as my grandmother's words were about Odd, they were nothing compared to the meal she had prepared for his memorial service.

I was pretty sure that if he had left any instructions behind about what to do when he died, hot dish would not have been something he asked for. Roasted meat fresh off the bone and plenty of mead, maybe, but definitely not ground meat mixed with frozen vegetables and cream of mushroom soup, topped with tater tots and lots of cheese.

He would've hated it. It spoke so much of my grandmother's place in Runde and not in Villmark. Which I'm sure is why she chose it.

I suspected Loke's hand in procuring the ingredients as well. He would appreciate the opportunity to get one last dig in against Odd Oddsen, for sure.

The heavy food was so soporific that when we were done eating and could only sit around the table, loaded down with carbs and cheese, the fact that our minds turned once more to the deceased and other dark topics felt completely natural.

"Do we know for a fact that he was intending to come into town and stir up trouble?" Brigida asked. "I mean, I know that fits his pattern. I don't doubt that was his motive. But just to be thorough, for posterity's sake."

"I don't think that was his plan at all, no," my grandmother said. "He came only this far south, and only to speak with me. He had sensed I was here, and that my powers had weakened."

"Was he angling for some advantage?" Valki asked.

"I don't think so. Believe it or not, I think he was just concerned. He and I did a little magic together, and he was satisfied with the results. He was planning to go back north, back out into the wilds, as soon as the ice storm passed. I think that was why he was so cross with Raggi and Báfurr for coming out here."

"What do you mean, he was satisfied with the results? Was he testing you?" Brigida asked.

"It always feels that way, doesn't it?" my grandmother said, and

Haraldr nodded a bit too vigorously. "Perhaps he meant to help. But his power is not the sort that bolsters mine. Ingrid and I have been slowly working back up to full strength over the last few days."

"The protection spells," Valki said.

"Yes. Ingrid was right, more protection was needed. But Villmark is safer now than it's ever been," she said.

"But also more in danger," Haraldr said. "We cannot deny that things are moving against us in a way they've never done in our history."

"Are Torfa's spells fading?" Brigida asked. A slight quaver to her voice betrayed the emotion she was fighting not to show.

But it was understandable. I was pretty sure everyone around the table was scared. I knew I was.

"I don't think so, but I'll be working to be certain of that fact over the next few weeks," my grandmother said. "It's going to be grueling."

"But you'll have your granddaughter to aid you," Haraldr said, not quite a question.

"No, Ingrid will be leaving soon," my grandmother said.

This was news to me. "Where am I going?" I asked.

"You'll be called away. But that's all right. You don't need to worry about me. I'll be just fine on my own now," she said.

"Will you be coming back into town?" Brigida asked.

"Not just yet," my grandmother said. "I need a little more time here on the shore. Then I'll come into Villmark to be closer to the ancestral fire. Assuming, of course, that I may use your house, Ingrid?"

"Of course," I said, a little stunned she felt she had to ask. It was really her house, as much as she loathed to use it.

"And Runde?" Haraldr asked.

"Definitely not just yet," my grandmother said. "My mead hall has an importance I know the three of you don't quite understand. It must be reopened, for the good of Villmark. But I'm not yet ready for the drain of it yet."

"How long am I going to be gone?" I asked.

"I have no idea, dear," my grandmother said.

"I think Runde must remain out of the question at least until your granddaughter returns," Brigida said firmly.

My grandmother closed her eyes for a moment, then nodded. I knew that wasn't a gesture of accepting the judgment of the council. Not remotely. She had just checked with whatever feeling had told her I was leaving and it had told her when I would be back.

My grandmother felt me watching her closely and gave me the smallest of winks.

Then there was a knock at the door, and I got up to answer it. I wasn't sure who it could be. As much as it was Wednesday, Valki had led the ox-cart with our supplies himself since it also contained Odd's body and Haraldr, who couldn't walk so far. So Loke and Roarr had the week off.

Unless Loke had changed his mind about waiting for me to talk to my grandmother first?

I was already formulating my responses to his questions. I had intended to bring it up with my grandmother, but all the spells we had been doing to protect Villmark had been more draining than she was letting the council see. Each night when we had finished our spell-work, I had tucked her into bed without having a moment to say anything to her at all, not even something as important as what was going on with Loke.

But when I opened the door, it wasn't Loke waiting on the doorstep.

It was Kara and Nilda.

And Kara looked like not only had she seen a ghost, but as if that ghost had sucked half the life out of here before she had gotten away. Her skin was paler than I had ever seen it, and her eyes were huge and haunted. Nilda had an arm around her, supporting her as if she couldn't stand on her own.

"We waited as long as we could," Nilda said, even as Kara slipped away from her to throw herself into my arms.

"We have to go," Kara said to me. "Promise me. Promise me we'll go."

"We'll go," I said.

Not that I had the slightest idea what I was agreeing to. But my grandmother already knew I was going, so it didn't matter. Whatever they told me next, I already knew I would agree to it.

But I had a pretty good idea what they were going to say. And going north to find Thorbjorn and Thorge was a mission I would drop everything else for in a heartbeat.

CHAPTER TWENTY-TWO

MY GRANDMOTHER CHASED the council out of the cabin even as Nilda
and I got a shivering Kara settled closer to our fireplace and stoked up
the fire to blaze uncomfortably hot. Valki wanted to object, or at least
wanted to know who was guarding the ancestral fire if all three of
them were there in Frór's cabin, miles away from that cave. But my
grandmother was insistent, and soon we were alone.

"Here," my grandmother said, putting a wooden mug of something
bitter-smelling into Kara's hands. She took a sip and grimaced, but my
grandmother lifted the bottom of the mug to be sure she drank it all.

Whatever it was, it stopped Kara's shivers in a way that the fire
hadn't.

"Now, tell me," my grandmother said.

"Did Ingrid tell you about my dreams?" Kara asked, her voice a
mere rasp.

"Only a little," my grandmother said, which was a lie. I hadn't told
her a bit of it yet.

So Kara explained it all to her, the feelings and then the dreams
and then the visions in the ancestral fire.

"Ingrid said not to look into the flames, and truly, I tried not to,"
Kara said.

"But you wanted to know," my grandmother said, squeezing both of Kara's hands in hers. "I understand. But you can see you've done some damage to yourself."

"How could I see anything in the flames if I'm not a volva?" she asked.

"Who ever told you that you're not a volva?" my grandmother asked.

Kara just blinked. "But isn't that just you? Your family line?"

"We may be the strongest, but we're not the only," my grandmother said. "Look at Halldis."

"Let's not," I said.

"We came here today because last night was the worst," Nilda said. "Kara was... well, it was scary. Like Wild Hunt scary. I can't have another night like that."

"You won't," my grandmother assured her.

"Something is after them. I just know it," Kara said, curling her hands into fists and pounding them into her thighs.

"I didn't see it," I said, and all three of them turned to give me puzzled looks. "Sorry, hold on," I said, and moved to my art corner to dig out the drawing I had done of Thorbjorn and Thorge in the mountain pass. I handed it to my grandmother, who examined it for a long time in very minute detail before letting Nilda and Kara put their heads together over it.

"Mjolner was with them," she said to me.

"At least for a time," I said. "Loke says Mjolner can go places he can't."

My grandmother just looked at me unblinkingly for a long beat, and I remembered I hadn't actually told her about Loke yet either. "One thing at a time," she said when I opened my mouth to explain. "When did you draw that sketch?"

"When I was in that fugue state, the night I spent in the Villmark house," I said. "My sketches led Loke and I to Báfurr, but there were also a bunch of sketches of Leifr and then this one of Thorbjorn and Thorge. And a ton of Loke too."

"Leifr," my grandmother said slowly, as if savoring the syllables of that name. "And Loke. Interesting. But one thing at a time."

"Thorbjorn and Thorge, then?" I asked.

"Yes. Why don't you sit down and draw again? See what happens when you're focused on just the one thing," she said. "Nilda and I will take Kara out for a little walk and some fresh air while you work."

"Thank you," I said.

I waited for the three of them to head out the door before facing the blank page. At first, I felt intimidated. I didn't know what I was drawing. I had no idea where to start. I could feel that feeling starting to snowball into a complete questioning of my abilities as an artist.

I closed my eyes and forced all those thoughts away. Then I took a deep breath, filling my lungs as full as they would go and then slowly letting it out again.

Inspiration.

And with that breath, the creative flow just started.

I heard the door bang open again some time later and stopped what I was doing, which seemed to be only adding more and more detail to the trunk of a tree on the side of a road. The warmth of the day was such that the three of them didn't have layers to shed when they came in. They were crowded around me to see what I drew even as I sat back to look at it myself.

"Thorbjorn and Thorge," I said. I had drawn them from behind in long cloaks, but I knew their postures well enough. Thorbjorn's locks were longer now, but the sides of Thorge's head were as clean-shaven as ever. Perhaps because I just loved to draw the tattoos he had curving over his ears.

"It's not a mountain pass now. It's just a road," Kara said. I looked back over my shoulder at her. Her voice had sounded stronger than before, but that was nothing compared to the transformation of her face. Her color was back, the hollows of her cheeks had filled in, and her eyes were back to their normal, nonhaunted size.

Whatever my grandmother had given her had really done the trick.

"What is that?" Nilda asked, pointing to something in the bottom lefthand side of the page.

I squinted at it. "It looks like a wagon," I said.

"It looks like it's glowing," Nilda said.

"I know that wagon," my grandmother said.

We all looked at her in surprise.

"Look, see the patterns traced on the side? I know that wagon," she said. There was a look on her face that I would swear was nostalgia. She was reminiscing on old memories, the good kind. The kind she hadn't had that morning for Odd.

"Whose wagon is it, mormor?" I asked.

"It belongs to a woman who calls herself Reginleif," she said. "She lives in it, forever traveling the old roads in the far north, never spending two nights in the same place."

"You've been in the far north?" I asked.

"When I was younger," my grandmother said.

"Is she from Villmark or somewhere else?" Nilda asked.

"Villmark originally," my grandmother said. "I'm sure of it, although she claims not to remember it at all."

"That's why you say she calls herself Reginleif? Because that's not the name her parents gave her?" I asked.

My grandmother's eyes sparkled at me. "Precisely. Reginleif was the name of one of the valkyries, and she took it as her own. It's one of her earliest memories, but she had thousands of years' worth of memories."

"How is that possible?" Kara asked.

But I was thinking something else. And my grandmother knew it. "Yes," she said, as if reading my mind. "Didn't you think it odd you kept drawing Leifr when you were trying to find Báfurr?"

"I thought he was my chief suspect for a long time," I admitted. "I thought I just had him too much on my mind. But you think that connects to this? This wagon?"

"Reginleif and Leifr? Are the names a coincidence?" Nilda asked, looking from me to my grandmother.

"Likely so," my grandmother said. "Leifr never forgot his own name, did he?"

"What are we talking about?" Kara asked.

"I don't suppose either of you ever met Leifr?" I said. They both shook their heads. "He wandered away from his family while hunting mushrooms as a boy. But it's impossible to say just how long he was gone. He said he disappeared at the age of nine, but he looks our age now. But according to the Book of the Settlement, he disappeared nearly two centuries ago."

"But in his mind it was thousands of years," my grandmother said. "And he kept the memory of his own name."

"So the same thing happened to this Reginleif, only she forgot her name?" Nilda asked. "Does that mean anything?"

"I think it means that out of all of them, Leifr might be the only one who stands a chance of rejoining life in Villmark. Reginleif knew it was beyond her capability, and so she wanders the roads to the north in her wagon, never to return to us."

"Out of all of them?" I said. "How many children have gone missing for thousands of years?"

"Maybe only three," my grandmother said and gave me a challenging look.

"Odd," I said. "The third one was Odd Oddsen."

"I think so," my grandmother said. "Like Reginleif, he chose his own name. He's never opened up to me, but I wouldn't be surprised if the moment he chose his name is the earliest of his memories."

"Is that why he seldom came back to Villmark and never to stay?" Kara asked. "Because he couldn't?"

"There have been others," my grandmother said. "If you look at the Book of the Settlement, you can count up the lost children, the ones who went into the woods and never returned. The ones who disappeared when their parents turned their backs for just the briefest of moments. Over the generations, there have been so many. But only three I know who came back in any form at all."

"How could that be true and no one ever speaks of it?" Kara asked. "Does that mean it doesn't happen anymore?"

"It's always a threat," my grandmother said, and gave me a look. "It was my greatest fear, when Ingrid was young. She glowed so brightly, so attractively, that the things that lurk in the wilds would never be able to resist her. And so I tried to keep her out of the wilds. But that failed too."

"I came back safe and sound," I said. "I was with Frór the whole time."

"And he never turned his back on you? Not even for a moment?"

I felt my cheeks flushing hot. Of course he had. Many times. And if that brief moment had been all that was required…

Maybe I was lucky to be where I was. Things could've ended very differently for me.

"So Thorbjorn and Thorge are with this friend of yours?" Kara asked, drawing our attention back to the sketch.

"At least we know they saw her," my grandmother said, moving across the room to dig into a little box on the mantlepiece. "I doubt they are still with her now, but she'll be able to point you in a direction for you to start."

"Once I find her," I said, not sure how we'd even start to do that.

"Here," my grandmother said, pressing an amulet into my palm and closing my hand over it.

"Magic?" I asked.

"No, just a token of friendship," she said. I opened my hand to see a little bronze spear. It looked like something a valkyrie would wield, I suppose. But my first thought was more that it was something a Native American might have carried on the Great Plains. But that was probably another coincidence. Spears only came in so many shapes, after all.

"Now, the three of you should get a move on if you're going to be in Villmark before sundown," my grandmother said briskly.

"Why am I going to Villmark?" I asked. That was in the exact opposite direction of wherever Reginleif might be.

"You have to pack for your journey," she said. "And *you* have to speak with Haraldr before you go. I'm sure he has another assignment for you before you leave on such a long mission."

I nodded, but my head was spinning. Why had she stressed the *you* like that? It sounded strange, but I couldn't put my finger on why.

"Then come back here and I'll give you a map," my grandmother went on. "It will take me that long to craft it. Maps to hidden territories are very hard to draw."

I suddenly thought of the map she had drawn for me, the one that had led me to Runde. As much as Runde was part of the mundane world, I hadn't been able to get there using my phone's navigation system. Only my grandmother's hand-drawn map.

"Very arduous work, so no need for the three of you to hurry back in the morning. Eat breakfast first, then have a stroll back up here, and then I should be ready."

I just nodded, my head still spinning from how fast everything was changing again.

But Kara noted what I had not.

"The three of us?" she said eagerly.

"Well, of course, the three of you," my grandmother said. "What did you think I meant when I said you all have to pack for your journey? Valki can put others on sentry duty over the ancestral fire. But Ingrid is going to need both of you with her to complete this task. And I have a feeling it will turn out to be more important even than you know."

"Getting Thorge home again is important enough for me," Kara said fiercely.

Nilda shot my grandmother a look of gratitude, then looked at her sister with worry in her eyes again. I'm sure she thought she was only going along to look out for her sister.

But I could tell that my grandmother meant what she said. Somehow, in the coming days, I was going to need the help of both of the Mikkelsen sisters.

And yet that didn't fill me with dread. Even the thought of going into the north wasn't scaring me in that moment.

I, like Kara, was just anxious to finally be doing what I realized I hadn't been letting myself think about how much I wanted to be doing for months now.

I was going to find Thorbjorn and bring him home safe again.

And no unseen, unknown menace was going to stop me.

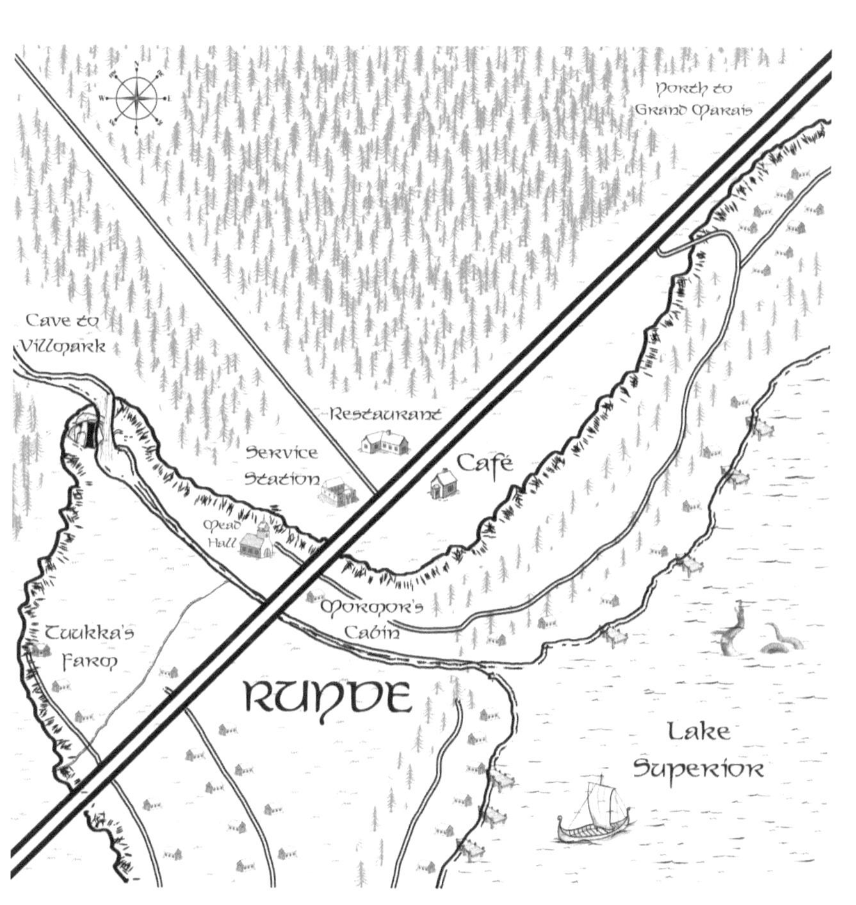

North to
Grand Marais
Cave to
Villmark
Restaurant
Service
Station
Café
Mead
Hall
Mormor's
Cabin
Tuukka's
Farm
RUNDE
Lake
Superior

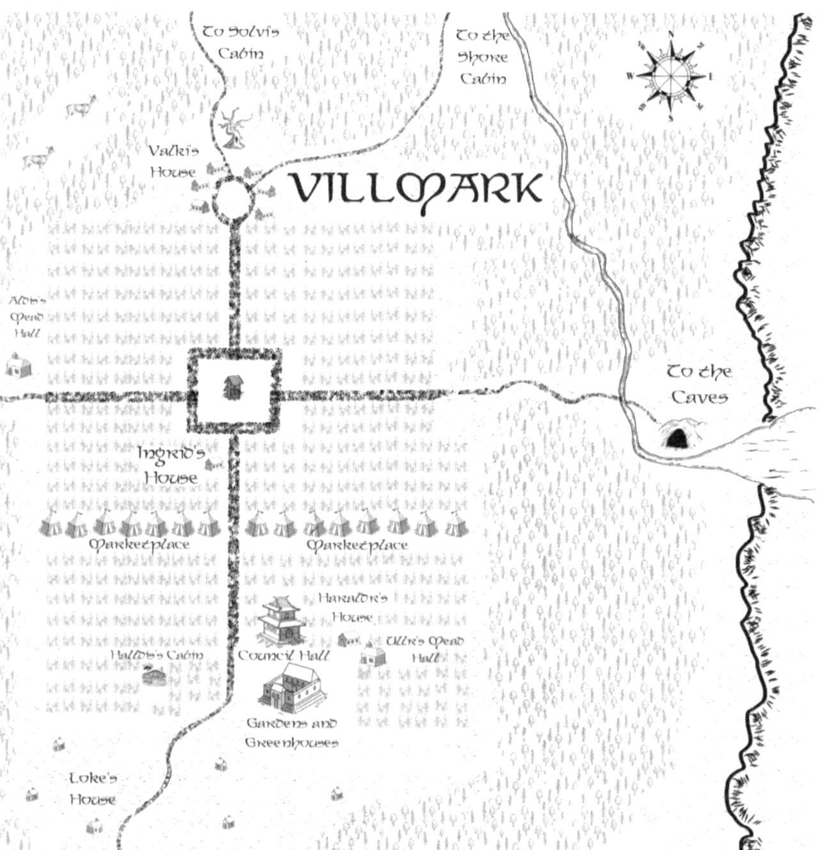
To Solvi's Cabin
To the Shore Cabin
N
S
E
W
Valki's House
VILLMARK
Aldis's Mead Hall
To the Caves
Ingrid's House
Marketplace
Marketplace
Harald's House
Ullr's Mead Hall
Halldis's Cabin
Council Hall
Gardens and Greenhouses
Loke's House

CHECK OUT BOOK EIGHT!

The Viking Witch will return in **Bones by the Forest Road**, available now!

Spring, the season of renewal, finally arrives on the North Shore of Lake Superior, and Ingrid Torfa finds herself in a strange new situation.

On vacation.

She and her grandmother spend their days resting and recuperating in an old cabin overlooking the shores of Lake Superior. She can see modern ships pass by along the shipping lanes on the horizon. But everything around her? Strictly from the Viking Age. Not even the lost Norse village of Villmark lies so far in the past as this lonely cabin.

But her restful vacation comes to a sudden end when a stranger knocks on their door. His presence disrupts their quiet lakeside lives even before he turns up dead.

Now Ingrid must figure out who wanted the strange old man dead. Because the next target just might be her.

Bones by the Forest Road, Book 8 in **The Viking Witch Mystery Series!**

THE WITCHES THREE
COZY MYSTERIES

In case you missed it, check out **Charm School**, the first book in the complete **Witches Three Cozy Mystery Series**!

Amanda Clarke thinks of herself as perfectly ordinary in every way. Just a small-town girl who serves breakfast all day in a little diner nestled next to the highway, nothing but dairy farms for miles around. She fits in there.

But then an old woman she never met dies, and Amanda was named in her will. Now Amanda packs a bag and heads to the big city, to Miss Zenobia Weekes' Charm School for Exceptional Young Ladies. And it's not in just any neighborhood. No, she finds herself on Summit Avenue in St. Paul, a street lined with gorgeous old houses, the former homes of lumber barons, railroad millionaires, even the writer F. Scott Fitzgerald. Why, Amanda can practically hear the jazz music still playing across the decades.

Scratch that. The music really, literally, still plays in the backyard of the charm school. Because the house stretches across time itself. Without a witch to protect this tear in the fabric of the world, anything can spill over. Like music.

Or like murder.

Charm School, the first book in the complete **Witches Three Cozy Mystery Series!**

THE WEAL & WOE BOOKSHOP
WITCH MYSTERIES

In case you missed it, check out **The Teashop Terror**, the first book in the complete **Weal & Woe Bookshop Witch Mystery Series**!

No one knows more about every branch of magic than Tabitha Greene. She devoted years to studying the most esoteric texts, hunting down the most obscure source materials, and deciphering the most cryptic ancient scrolls. But her career in academia hits a dead end when no wizard will take her on as an apprentice.

Just because, despite being descended from two long and prestigious lines of witches, her attempts to actually perform any magic always fail. Often spectacularly.

But no more college means no more dorm life. And no magical skills means no real job skills, at least, not in the witchy world. And a life spent moving from school to school every few months was a life without real friendships. She finds herself alone with nowhere to go.

Then an uncle she barely remembers offers her a summer job, running his bookstore over the summer. The Weal and Woe Bookstore, located in a magical pocket world within a block of buildings just north of the old Mill District of Minneapolis, Minnesota.

Not exactly the pinnacle of all her hopes and dreams. But it's just for one summer, right?

Or so Tabitha tells herself. But unbeknownst to her, the Weal and Woe Bookstore is about to change her life.

The Teashop Terror, the first book in the complete **Weal & Woe Bookshop Witch Mystery Series**!

The Ritchie and Fitz Sci-Fi Murder Mysteries starts with **Murder on the Intergalactic Railway**.

For Murdina Ritchie, acceptance at the Oymyakon Foreign Service Academy means one last chance at her dream of becoming a diplomat for the Union of Free Worlds. For Shackleton Fitz IV, it represents his last chance not to fail out of military service entirely.

Strange that fate should throw them together now, among the last group of students admitted after the start of the semester. They had once shared the strongest of friendships. But that all ended a long time ago.

But when an insufferable but politically important woman turns up murdered, the two agree to put their differences aside and work together to solve the case.

Because the murderer might strike again. But more importantly, solving a murder would just have to impress the dour colonel who clearly thinks neither of them belong at his academy.

Murder on the Intergalactic Railway, the first book in **The Ritchie**

and Fitz Sci-Fi Murder Mysteries, available everywhere books are sold.

FREE EBOOK!

Like exclusive, free content?

If you'd like to receive "A Collection of Witchy Prequels", a free collection of short story prequels to the Witches Three Cozy Mystery and Viking Witch Mystery series, as well as other free stories throughout the year, go to my website CateMartin.com to subscribe to my newsletter! This eBook is exclusively for newsletter subscribers and will never be sold in stores. Check it out!

ABOUT THE AUTHOR

Cate Martin has written stories which have appeared in **Mystery, Crime and Mayhem** quarterly magazine as well as in the annual **Holiday Spectacular** Advent calendar of Christmas stories. She is also the author of three witch mystery series: **The Witches Three Cozy Mysteries**, and **The Viking Witch Mysteries** and **The Weal and Woe Bookshop Witch Mysteries**. She currently lives in Minneapolis, Minnesota. You can learn more about her work at CateMartin.com.

ALSO BY CATE MARTIN

The Witches Three Cozy Mystery Series

Charm School

Work Like a Charm

Third Time is a Charm

Old World Charm

Charm his Pants Off

Charm Offensive

The Witches Three Cozy Mysteries Books 1-3

The Witches Three Cozy Mysteries Books 4-6

The Viking Witch Mystery Series

Body at the Crossroads

Death Under the Bridge

Murder on the Lake

Killing in the Village Commons

Bloodshed in the Forest

Corpse in the Mead Hall

Slaying on the Lake Shore

Bones by the Forest Road

Sacrifice Behind the Falls

Body Under the Café

Assassination in the Glade

Bewitchment After the Storm

Predator in the Lanes

Threat From the North

Snare in the Blind Alley

Ashes Beneath the Tree (available July 14, 2026 direct from me or August 11, 2026 in stores everywhere)

The Viking Witch Mysteries Books 1-3

The Viking Witch Mysteries Books 4-6

The Viking Witch Mysteries Books 7-9

The Weal & Woe Bookshop Witch Mystery Series

The Teashop Terror

The Salon & Spa Scandal

The Bookseller Blunder

The Entrepreneur Enigma

The Novelty Shop Nightmare

The Courtyard Conundrum

Short Story Collections

Bubbly, Bicycles and Brides

The Dorothy Lundegaard Mysteries

Fruitcake, Festivities and Firelight